MW01170395

Chickens and Mosquitoes
The Art of Uncertain Times

by Carol K. Psaros

ISBN 978-1-62806-058-4

Library of Congress Control Number 2014960309

Published by Salt Water Media
29 Broad Street, Suite 104
Berlin, Maryland 21811
www.saltwatermediallc.com

Cover painting by artist Jack Lewis, "Mosquito Control, Lewes, 1936" is oil on canvas, used with permission from the U. S. National Archives and Records Administration and the Delaware Division of Historical and Cultural Affairs. The chicken painting on the back cover is an unpublished watercolor by artist Jack Lewis and is used with permission from the Delaware Division of Historical and Cultural Affairs, Heather Lewis, and Sally Lewis Sharpless.

Dedicated to the men of the Civilian Conservation Corps, and to the resiliency of the human spirit wherever it is found.

In 1940 N. C. Wyeth wrote in his Introduction to Jack Lewis' book *The Delaware Scene*, "it is an especial solace and stimulation to come upon such pictures as are presented in this book by this young and sensitive artist, Mr. Jack Lewis. His paintings are modest and unassuming and are born of sincerity and great sympathy. This collection of reproductions from the original water colors offers to anyone of discernment a glimpse into the artist's heart, and through it an appealing record of a section of the land, the people, and the villages he loves."

Introduction
By Heather Lewis

Nearly forty years ago I left my childhood home in southern Delaware for art school in Philadelphia, then a decade or so to be in Central New York to begin my family. However, tide water runs in my veins, and the old familiar tug of marshland and the watery world of the Atlantic Ocean pulled me to coastal Maine where I have lived ever since. But today, I am in the car with my youngest daughter, Lucy, making the journey back to Rehoboth, Delaware for a family reunion and memorial art show for my father, the late artist, Jack Lewis.

It's a long trek from North Berwick, Maine, and we've been driving south for six hours leaving the cooler, drier hills of New England far behind us. The air outside the air conditioned car is hot and sticky. This land is flat now -low country. It is lush, green farm land, with corduroy like rows of soy beans, and corn. Once over the St. George's Bridge, every hypnotic mile is a count backwards on my memory's clock. Sitting between my daughter and me, my long dormant childhood wakes up, shakes its sleepy head, and with astonishing accuracy, points out landmarks. This trip is turning out to be a sentimental journey across these familiar Delaware scenes.

And as we get closer, both Lucy and I can feel my father's presence with us, too, and she indulges me as I reminisce: *Being the surprise baby to middle aged parents, I was often my dad's pal and sidekick; my mother being understandably more interested in my teen aged sister's business. As he sought out picturesque places to paint, there I'd be, co-piloting from the passenger seat of our Rambler station wagon, classical music on the radio, criss-crossing farmland in lower Delaware and Maryland's Eastern Shore.*

My father's quest for the perfect scene could get very boring, with only the promise of our ritual Dairy Queen ice cream cone barely quieting my fidgety little girl self. Finding the location was just part of it, though. After going along never ending back roads, my snack already eaten, and all my packed-up toys and games played with and discarded - he still had to search for the perfect view. This was nearly painful. We'd creep along the roadside, going backwards and forwards, my dad holding his hands up in front of one of his eyes, squinting, making a little picture window in search of the perfect "composition", whatever that was. Finally, we'd end up at what he deemed the perfect spot: some obscure back water, which, even to me, seemed somewhat pleasant. Another little estuary, alongside a marsh, with a couple of old boats, and remarkably, seemingly out of nowhere, some long lost friend from the CCC days would mysteriously appear, and provide a bit of "human interest" to the scene.

On the road way we go over bridges and there's

no sleeping for my memories now. The years away from this place disappear. We pass Leipsic, and Lucy recognizes the place she's grown up seeing every day in one of her grandfather's paintings which hung in her childhood home. "Mom, is that the place in that little painting we have from Grampa? I always thought it was called Lipstick!" I feel my heart beat, and then closer to Dover, with signs for Little Creek and Port Mahon, it beats even faster still. Bowers Beach, Magnolia, Frederica, Nassau. It's all coming back to me now- I am a native of this slow, fertile farm country by the ocean. Mile after mile of giant metal structures on wheels, irrigation systems, misting hundreds of acres of crops making small low hanging rainbows arc over the fields. This is a magical place. And there are the things that I remember and love most of all, the beautiful, timeless marshes, whose sentinel like cat tails guard its edges, and lazy grasses finger the slow moving current as its makes its way to the bay. Lucy announces : "We're almost there, Mom!", and I look out the window, across the expanse of marshland, and see a giant windmill dominating the landscape. With one eye squinted, I look through a little frame I make with my hands and search for the perfect view, but, there are so many.

Chickens and Mosquitoes, The Art of Uncertain Times, is a time capsule, which tells us about life in southern Delaware during the last century, particularly during the Great Depression of the 1930's. Author, Carol K. Psaros, gifts the reader with first hand stories, including those from her father, the late Jim Kelley, and by my father the late Jack Lewis. Our fathers were CCC men who became friends nearly eighty years ago when they were assigned to a mosquito control camp in Lewes, Delaware. My father was an artist in the CCC camp, and Mr. Kelley was his supervisor. I was moved as the character of my father as a young man came alive, and I could actually picture him creating the paintings which hung in my childhood home, and now are part of the State of Delaware's collection. An intimate look into the lives of gentle, resourceful and hard-working folk, we learn how people came together and lived productive and prosperous lives during challenging and most definitely "uncertain times".

Heather Lewis and daughter Lucy

CHAPTER ONE

Obstacles… like windy weather… are good for resolution. In the wind a painter can only be concerned with the essential features of the subject.

- Jack Lewis

Jim held the letter and realized that his hands were shaking. His youngest brother Bobby had run the envelope to him as soon as the postman left the front porch.

"Dear Sir: I have the honor to inform you that you have been selected for appointment as a cadet of the United States Military Academy at West Point, N.Y., contingent upon the failure of the principal candidate and the first alternate from the at-large Congressional district of Delaware to quality for admission….." Jim stopped breathing and read the sentence again. And again. It continued to say the same thing.

He had finished third, not even second, as it so

clearly indicated at the top of the August 31, 1927 letter from the Adjutant General's Office of the WAR DEPARTMENT. The remainder of the letter blurred in his vision and a single tear fell onto the one page catastrophe.

A military career had been his strongest dream ever since being selected to join the Bellmen at Laurel High. Jim appreciated the discipline and regimen the quasi-military group demanded, in contrast to the chaos at home. Between his five younger brothers and one older sister, there was always an argument underway. As a Bellman, Jim had attended two week Citizen Military Training Camps at Plattsburg, N.Y. the summers before his junior and senior years. Both summer camps were like brief vacations, tent adventures with the Adirondack Mountains and the rapids and flume of the Ausable Chasm for a backdrop. The clear mountain air had made him feel strong and believe that a career in the Army should be his life's work.

Hadn't his credentials been sufficient? Perhaps there had been a mistake. Throughout high school he had been a leader, Vice-President of his Senior Class, honor roll student, President of one of the two literary societies, Captain of the baseball team and one of its leading hitters, lineman on the football team, Business Editor and reporter for the school newspaper. On Senior Class Day, he wrote and read an eleven page *"Last Will and Testament for the Class of 1926"* that Jim thought would have made his hero Abraham Lincoln proud. Jim bound the epistle in green and gold ribbons, the class colors, and pasted an official looking seal "Of Guaranteed Quality" on its cover. In ink on parchment paper, applying his beautiful cursive, he penned a preamble for the twenty-four item bequest:

Cutting so rapidly loose from life and finding so many things of such gigantic proportions to be attended to before the end should come upon her, realizing at the same time that she had no longer any time left to spend in cultivation of her own virtues, she did collectively and individually deem it best to distribute these virtues with her own hands to those friends to whose needs they seem best fitted. As a result of this, I do hereby make, publish, and declare this as the last will and testament of the said graduating class.

Jim was also intrigued with theatrical arts. Often he would work extra odd jobs around the neighborhood so he could afford to see a local stage production. Jim wanted a speaking part in his Senior Class Play, "Captain Cross Bones," but he had to settle for serving as advertising coordinator and being in the play's chorus because of after school work and athletics. Secretly, he wrote poems and tore them up so his brothers would not find them. He read every novel and historical essay he could obtain free in the school or town library. He loved military history the most, especially the Civil War.

What had gone wrong? Certainly, he knew that there was nothing lacking in his physique or personality. At 6'2" he was the tallest in his class and looked like a poster for the War Department in his

Bellman uniform. His many male buddies liked him as a person and envied his ability to handle academics and athletics with natural earnestness, if not ease.

As the reality of the rejection letter took hold, Jim felt a cold depression surround him. This was not his first disappointment. After graduating from Laurel High, he had not received *any* letter from the War Department, although he had requested academy appointments through all the proper channels. His parents were determined to gather enough funds to send him to Blackstone Military Academy in Blackstone, Virginia. So he settled for a year of college preparation with emphasis on securing math and engineering courses that had not been available at Laurel H.S., and on widening his military experience.

Blackstone Academy was a year in paradise. The Shenandoah Valley was beautiful beyond description. He excelled in the regimen and the academics, and found the esprit de corps to be exhilarating. There was a glorious order and schedule to everything, and on June 5, 1927, he graduated with academic, athletic, and conduct honors. He had achieved high marks in Solid Geometry, Trigonometry, Surveying, and French II. While playing football and baseball, he compiled an academic average of 93, the second highest among the 140 cadets. Jim was Salutatorian of his Blackstone Academy class which was five times as big as his 1926 Laurel High graduating class. He had done exceptionally well.

To help repay his parents for their financial support of his year at Blackstone, he worked three different summer jobs. He felt good about bringing home money to his mother who smiled with pride whenever he did. His father's brakeman salary with the Pennsylvania Railroad was reliable, but not extensive for a family of nine. Now Jim felt like he was fully prepared to enter West Point and begin his military career.

But it was August now, and the letter, the terrible letter, was still in his hand. Jim focused his bleary eyes and read, "Should the principal candidate and the first alternate fail to qualify, and should it be found that you possess the qualifications required by law and regulations, you will be admitted to the Academy, without further examination, upon reporting in person to the Superintendent at West Point...." As much as he wanted to believe otherwise, Jim knew that scenario was fantasy.

There was very little time to feel sorry for himself. Another academic year was about to begin. His parents, his sister, and his five brothers, often looked away when he entered the room. The day after he received the letter, his mother came into his bedroom, sat on his bed, and said, "Son, I pray that the Lord will ease your anger and restore your spirit soon." His father, as usual, was stoically silent, although Jim could see a glint of sadness, or was it anger, in his father's eyes whenever their eyes met. Laurel Superintendent, Major C. A. Schoot, visited Jim's home in Delmar to try to console him and to help him think about his September plans. Colonel A.E. Tanner, the originator of the Laurel High Bellmen, telephoned him from his new job at Ferris School for Boys in Wilmington, Delaware, and gave him words of encouragement. Telephone calls were rare on the party line that the Kelley family shared with the Dashield family next door. Everyone's sympathy was somewhat sustaining, but Jim still felt like a failure.

The one image that seemed to calm Jim's heart was melancholy face of Abraham Lincoln in Jim's U.S. History book, as the President struggled with the blood and destruction of the Civil War. If Lincoln could remain strong after the death of his young son and the destruction of his beloved country, certainly Jim could learn how to live with his demons. Without the financial backing of the United States military, it would be harder to secure a college education, but he was determined to do it. He was young, resourceful, and strong of mind and body. He would find a way somehow. Perhaps it didn't matter that he would not have a military career.

Earlier Jim had been contacted by alumni of the University of Richmond and by Gettysburg College who liked his academic and military record, but really wanted him for his football and baseball skills. In the end, it was a family decision to send him to Randolph Macon College in Ashland, Virginia. Randolph Macon had suggested a deferred payment plan that could be met with his father's Christmas bonus in December. Three of his four brothers were able to work, Bobby being too young, and Francis too sickly; and they all decided to donate their odd job money to the family college fund for Jim and his sister Ruth, who was entering her sophomore year at the University of

Delaware.

Several of Jim's classes at Randolph Macon were a repeat of the Blackstone credits, so unexpectedly, as a freshman, he had time for himself. He loved browsing in the library stacks, playing tennis on Sunday afternoons, and seeing plays on campus or in a nearby town, if he could hitch a ride. When the football team traveled to Gettysburg College, he visited the historic battlefield where the Delaware militia had made their charge up Pickett's Hill. Even with days of football practices and games, he had time to become a social member of Kappa Alpha Fraternity. Everyone liked him, but it humbled Jim that his fraternity brothers were willing to call him a "pledge" even though he could not pay his initiation dues. In his spring semester, two of his classmates hired him to tutor them in English literature and geometry. More than anyone, Jim knew that college was a privilege for him, and a sacrifice for his family, and he gave thanks for every day of learning.

At home during the summer of 1928, he worked like a migrant to earn money. The economy was stagnant and even part-time jobs were very hard to come by. Nearly everyone in Delmar had been approached by one of the Kelley boys who offered to cut the grass, paint a fence, or fix a window. Since he had been away from home two years, he had lost many of his local contacts. And because his brothers had so generously supported him, he did not want to cut into their territory. So Jim rode his bike to local farms and picked strawberries, blueberries, peaches, cantaloupe and corn. Anytime he saw migrant workers, he would seek the field boss and beg a job. Usually he got paid. By a fluke, he was hired for two weeks, to substitute for a friend who was hurt while pitching tar on the county roads. That money was a windfall. At night he did the books for Dr. Prettyman, M.D. who lived down the street. Every penny went into the family college fund, and he joyfully returned to Ashland late summer for football camp.

College life was even better as a sophomore. He was able to elect European History and British Literature, and spring semester he planned to take a course in Shakespeare and a philosophy course. But at Christmas break when Jim returned home, silence and sadness greeted him. He could see the pathetic look in his parents' eyes, and the "heart to heart" reality came as soon as Christmas day ended. His father did all the talking this time, while his mother sat holding a handkerchief beside him. Quite formally, his father said, "James, it pains me to tell you that we won't be able to support your return to college. Francis needs an operation in two weeks, and my Christmas bonus this year will be used for his surgery. I am truly sorry. His mother stifled a sob, but Jim took the news like the military man he still wanted to be. It was a relief in a way not to feel like he was causing his whole family stress. Jim had the presence of mind to say, "I understand completely," and then mumble, "I'll take the semester off and work until I can pay my own way." He hugged his mother and told her it would be all right.

The new year of 1929 came roaring into Delmar with

a snow storm, and Jim went right to work shoveling driveways. But being home was tedious after two and a half years of independence, and he was just another mouth for his parents to feed. There were plenty of hands to help around the house without him. He had to find another place to live.

By February he had moved in with his sister, Ruth, who was living off campus in Newark, Delaware and sharing rent with another woman. Ruth was already a junior, and she had earned most of her in-state tuition for the University of Delaware waiting tables at Rehoboth Beach the summer before. Jim had the corner of the small living room as "his area" and the couch at night. His long frame had to curl up to snooze on the sofa, and some nights the floor was more comfortable and reminiscent of the army cots at Plattsburg, N.Y. Sharing the bathroom with two women was an educational experience he had not been afforded at Randolph Macon or Blackstone. Having been around men for so long, it was refreshing to see the world from a woman's viewpoint. Ruth was a feisty redhead with a big smile and large white teeth, just like his. She was a decisive personality and had a knack for going after just what she wanted. Ruth and her roomie told him he could use their place as his "headquarters" while he job hunted in the greater Newark-Wilmington-Philadelphia area. He felt like he was a squatter, but he was determined to swallow his pride and keep focused on the prize of a college education.

Every morning he scanned the newspapers

then walked the streets, stopping by the University's placement office to see if he qualified for any of the postings, which were not numerous. He set up his work post in the living room and sent our ten or more letters each day with his qualifications enclosed. He landed a job as a night watchman at a Newark factory, and by summer he secured three different part-time jobs as a lifeguard at the University swim center, as a janitor at a church, and as a clerk in a department store. His earnings were divided into his college account, a food-rent payment to his sister, and an amount sent home to his parents each month.

Then October 1929 arrived, and everything changed overnight. Financial collapse of the banks and the widespread loss of credit closed businesses and destroyed dreams. Jim was let go from his night watchman, clerk, and janitor jobs. With only the three hours of lifeguarding at the University pool on Saturdays, he had essentially no income. Worse, he'd received a letter from his mother telling him that his chronically ill brother, Francis, had to be institutionalized because of his deteriorating health. Just as unsettling were rampant rumors that his father's pension with the Pennsylvania Railroad might be gone.

Jim, ever the Abraham Lincoln realist, kept a positive attitude at first. But he failed to comprehend the effect the economic collapse would have on employment. In a month or so, as he saw the ranks of the jobless grow like a cancer, he grew alarmed. There were no job openings of any type to apply for, anywhere. Now, not only was college at stake, but his ability to provide for his own food and shelter was in doubt. Returning home was not an option, nor was staying in his sister's apartment any longer.

CHAPTER TWO

The trait of individuality, realism — being as one is — becomes more and more precious and lovable as one sees these people of the elements.

- Jack Lewis

Best friends Carolyn Brogan and Virginia Eggleston were huddled in whispers on the large porch. "I just can't do it, Ginny." Carolyn whimpered, quite uncharacteristically, embroidered hankie in hand. "She just doesn't understand why I don't want to marry him. Really, I don't understand it either, but it's unthinkable right now." Sniffle. "This afternoon when I came home from swimming laps at the Swim Club, Mother wouldn't even look at me as I walked past her bridge ladies in the dining room." Sniffle. "Since I've been home this Easter break, the tension between us has been horrid! She just can't accept that I'm not going to become engaged and marry Homer after we graduate."

"It's not like this is a quick decision," Virginia, ever the understanding friend said softly. "You've been like a pacing tiger the last six months trying to decide what to do, or more correctly, how to do it gracefully." How true. Virginia always knew her better than Carolyn knew herself. They had been together since kindergarten, and now they were about to graduate from Ohio Wesleyan University. Virginia understood how hard it had been for Carolyn to travel from the O.W.U. campus in Delaware, Ohio to Dayton to tell Homer in person. They had met their freshman year and became "pinned" the next spring. Joyfully and faithfully, they had supported each other through every moment of learning and growing, and Homer was truly a good person. He had a fine mind and a kind heart, everything a woman could want in a husband. The visit with Homer and his Mother, whom Carolyn was particularly fond of, did not go well, as expected from a "I'm not going to marry you" encounter. First there was silence, then shouting, then tears. But for Carolyn, the hardest assignment was coming home for Easter and telling her parents, Elsie and Charles Brogan, that she wasn't going to marry Homer. It was almost mandatory, after all. Sniffle.

The friends did not speak for a long time as they held hands listening to the rain drops that had begun to fall softly outside on the patio of the expansive lawn. The Brogan home was a newly built stately stone Tudor on a corner lot at Guernsey and Thayer roads in Swarthmore, Pennsylvania. Charles Brogan owned Shipley Machine Tools, which had been a financial success thanks to his expertise and the country's manufacturing boom after the "Great War." Carolyn and her brother Charles had not wanted for anything growing up, and both were excellent golfers, tennis players, and swimmers. Charles was nine years younger, so they ran in different circles now, but Carolyn adored her "little brother" who she had mothered since he was born.

"Ginny, what am I going to do now?" Carolyn finally broke the silence. "You have your teaching job at Pottstown High School all lined up, and I am still uncommitted." 'Uncommitted,' the word sounded like a prison sentence, something akin to 'unwilling to marry and not certain of anything'. "Virginia, I hardly recognize myself. You know how I'm always sure of what I want and how to get there. Now it seems like my world is wide open and I'm tripping at the threshold."

Out of the silence Virginia whispered, "Did you ever think that your abundant talents are making it difficult? You are intelligent, educated, beautiful, and an exceptional athlete, not to mention stupid enough to try anything once. Remember when you convinced the gondolier in Venice to oar us to a hidden alcove so you could take a dip in the canal?" she giggled. "Carolyn, be thankful that you can do almost anything fairly well, and many things very well, and trust that the answers will reveal themselves. You will know what to do when the time comes. You always do."

Sweet Virginia, always encouraging, ever the

adult. The rain drops were pounding down now on the canvas awnings of the porch and the sweet smell of spring whisked through the screens. With a deep breath, Carolyn surveyed her options. "Well the time is now to act on this graduate school acceptance and the two job inquiries I've received. Even though I might like to have more time, it's April and people want a commitment." There was that word again. The letter from Temple University's graduate school said she was admitted to the College of Social Sciences and asked her to contact her assigned Faculty Advisor to select courses towards a defined major. If she did so immediately, she could begin her graduate program during the summer. While in college, Carolyn had enjoyed spending part of each summer working with youth at a suburban Philadelphia community center. She taught them how to swim and how to improve their writing skills. But Carolyn realized she required more courses in psychology and sociology, and needed some targeted internships to become an effective social worker.

The second letter in the pile Carolyn held in her lap was from Glen Nor High School in Glenolden, Pennsylvania, where she had excelled as a student athlete, graduating with academic honors and setting scoring records as Captain of the girls' basketball team. Her alma mater was very interested in her returning in September to teach sophomore English classes and coach the girls' intermural basketball and field hockey teams. They would be delighted if she would find the time to start an intramural girls' tennis program as well. However, her calculated salary would be just for teaching English, with the coaching duties an unpaid, but expected, assignment.

The other teaching offer from a high school in Selbyville, Delaware was on the bottom of the pile. It was similar to the Glen Nor proposal, but with a significantly lower salary. However, she would be paid a small stipend for each team she coached. The Delaware high school had written in response to a letter the Ohio Wesleyan Placement Office had circulated, and it came surprisingly unsolicited. Selbyville High School requested that she appear in person on Monday, June 15, for a job interview.

"Virginia, can you believe that tomorrow's all day train ride to Columbus will be our last together? We've seen each other nearly every day our whole lives, and changing that is going to be so strange. I'm ready to leave college, but facing my shaky future without you is dreary, dearie."

"I feel the same way about leaving you, but let's not get locker room shakes like we did before we crushed Merion in the finals. I promise to write you from Pottstown every week because new hires often have time on their hands."

"Ginny, you know what hurts the most? Understanding that Mother really wants me to marry Homer now and have babies. We would attend the Presbyterian Church and then have Sunday lunch at the Ingelnuk. I could be a proper married woman and eventually join her bridge club. But life, I think, shouldn't be so scripted. Besides, Virginia, I don't want babies. I want my own basketball team."

Two months later, Carolyn peered over the steering wheel of the shiny blue Buick. It was a big automobile that purred across the smooth new pavement of the DuPont Highway. Upon graduation, her Father had presented her with the keys to the family car, giving her parents a good reason to buy the latest model.

As she drove, Carolyn realized how much she missed her weekly letter from Homer and his occasional phone calls. She appreciated his sharp sense of humor and his complete devotion to her. Carolyn let out a gentle sign, as some pangs of guilt made her shoulders sag. But an instant later, thoughts of Homer evaporated with the adventure of youthful independence.

The drive from Swarthmore, PA to Selbyville, DE was projected to take five hours, but Carolyn wanted to allow extra time in case she got lost. So far, so good. She had traveled south to Smyrna, DE and stopped for a delicious lunch at the Wayside Inn. The new DuPont Highway was beautiful and just went straight away south for miles. As she passed the State Capital in Dover, and then the towns of Greenwood and Harrington, the land became entirely flat so she had perfect visibility in all directions. Compared to driving in suburban Philadelphia, this was a walk in the park.

Selbyville High School had made a reservation for her to stay overnight at a boarding house across the street from the school. Thus she had until 9:00 a.m. tomorrow to present herself for the job interview. As she drove, Carolyn felt comfortable with her decision. If the interview went badly, she could still enroll in graduate school in September. Going back to her old high school was her third choice because the script seemed too fixed. And living at home was not an option. As Virginia had predicted, she had known what she wanted when the time came.

As she drove, signs and an occasional stop light signaled the arrival of each town. She dutifully observed the reduced speed as she entered each town limits. Streets were clean and many homes were stately with covered front porches. Outside of town, the never ending flat farmland was filled with corn and other crops, cows, a few horse farms, a peach orchard in Bridgeville, and lots of barns. Nothing was crowded, and even in town, houses had good sized lawns between them.

When she arrived in Selbyville after only asking for directions once, she noticed that the town was larger than some of the others she had traveled through. She passed a church, the bank, and the post office, and turned onto Hosier Street. Then she gasped in delight! Before her was the most gorgeous three story brick school building she had ever seen. It appeared to be brand new, and according to the sign, it was. Quickly, she pulled into the parking space for the Hudson Boarding House, switched off the ignition, and jumped out just to stare. She blinked and tried to take it all in. The school sat back from the street on a large expanse of property. A wide semi-circular drive was beautifully landscaped, although many of the plantings were new. And in the center of the front lawn was a huge flag pole with colors flying. Behind the building, although obstructed from her view, Carolyn was certain there would be a track and athletic fields. It was picture perfect, like a postcard.

That night Carolyn found it hard to sleep, so she jotted off a note to Virginia. In the morning, she took a quick two block walk and dropped the letter into the mail slot at the Selbyville Post Office. A man was painting a wall mural inside the Post Office and she stood for a moment to see that he was creating a farm scene of a man feeding chickens. It was a far cry from the masterpiece frescos she had seen in Venice, but she was pleasantly surprised that contemporary art was evident in southern Delaware---and in the Post Office, of all places.

At nine o'clock sharp she walked across the street to the High School. It was so simple. No trains or trolleys required. She was wearing her favorite seersucker suit, white blouse, and navy heels, and she felt "smashing." The Secretary announced her arrival, and Principal Thomas Howie came swiftly out of his office to greet her and usher her to a designated seat at the conference table. Carolyn was introduced to Hazel Scotton, senior English teacher, Frank Garber, physical educator and football coach, and Janet Parsons, mathematics teacher. Principal Howie was seated to Carolyn's left at the head of the table.

"Thank you for making the trip south for this interview. I hope your drive from Philadelphia was uneventful."

"It was quite pleasant and without incident."

"Good, so glad you are here. We are interviewing

today for a dual assignment in English and Physical Education with extra coaching duties. You would teach 9-12 grade physical education and health classes, and two sections of 9th grade English. Ohio Wesleyan has forwarded us your fine academic transcript and attached a description of your athletic achievements in basketball, swimming, field hockey, and golf. On paper, you appear to be very qualified for this job, which is why we are all here today. After we ask you some questions, Miss Parsons will give you a tour of our building, including the gymnasium and our athletic fields behind the school. Do you have any questions before we begin?"

"Was this beautiful building just built?"

"Yes, it was completed in March, and we had the official ribbon cutting in May, but students arrive here for the first time after Labor Day. The whole town is excited about our new state-of-the-art facility. Now could you tell us why you think you would be the best person we could hire for this job?"

Carolyn was a bit struck by the direct nature of his question, but she had been well drilled in interview techniques by the OWU Placement Office. "Yes, as a teacher and a coach, I would bring youth and enthusiasm to any learning moment. While teaching writing skills to Philadelphia youth, I discovered that I'm most alive when I'm around young people. They are challenging, and they make me laugh. I think my double major in Physical Education and English, and my demonstrated athletic strengths, are just what you are looking for."

Mr. Garber described the high school curriculum for girls' physical education classes and explained the school's policy on gym suits and showers. It was pretty much standard practice. He asked her if these were policies she could support, and she said "yes." Mrs. Scotton asked Carolyn who were her favorite British and American authors and asked her to give an example of how she would teach a unit on each. Carolyn thought she answered the question adequately because Mrs. Scotton's eyes sparkled as she listened to Carolyn explain how she would make Milton's *Paradise Lost* meaningful for ninth graders and then quoted from Whitman's. "I hear America Singing."

Principal Howie closed the meeting by talking about the Selbyville community. He handed Carolyn a booklet with pictures of the Mayor, and the members of the School Board. Selbyville, he said, was growing in population in spite of the recent depression. He wanted Carolyn to know that it was an ordinary town with extraordinary people who looked after each other. He thanked her again and said he would let her know the outcome of the interview very soon.

Once outside the Principal's office, Miss Parsons asked Carolyn to call her "Jan." They chatted amicably as she was shown the cafeteria, her potential Homeroom, 9B, where she would teach her two English classes, and the gymnasium with its girls' locker room and showers. Every area was pristine and had the smell of new paint and gleamed with abundant lighting. The classrooms were spacious with large windows for great ventilation. The gymnasium was large and multipurpose, allowing separate areas for boys and girls, with a folding door evenly dividing the space. The center of the gym floor glistened with shellac protecting the school mascot at center court. In an instant, Carolyn visualized her players poised around the center circle as the referee tossed the first jump ball of the season. Her girls, her team.

As they walked outside in the slightly warm June sunlight, Carolyn surveyed the track and football field with its abundant bleachers. Jan Parsons pointed behind the bleachers to the newly sodded hockey field with its netted goal cages. Amazingly there were two tiers of bleachers situated midfield on each sideline. Would there be fans, for girls' sports, Carolyn wondered? Carolyn could see a new softball diamond on the land beyond the hockey field. It was all just like a postcard.

Janet Parsons shared that she had recently taken up golf, and would love the chance to play a round with Carolyn should she be the candidate hired. "How nice it would be to have another female golfer in Selbyville," Jan confided.

Driving home, Carolyn pondered it all. Was life supposed to be this easy? She had imagined a rural school in depression disrepair, and instead, she had found the picture perfect place. The contract terms were exactly what the school had advertised, $1,500 with $75 stipends for coaching the interscholastic girls' basketball and field hockey teams.

That morning, Carolyn was surprised to find Principal Howie enjoying a cup of coffee in her boarding house dining room when she came down for breakfast. "Miss, Brogan, I'd like to offer you the job for your consideration. The committee was unanimous in wanting you to become a member of our faculty. Our school board Chairman, Clayton Bunting, approved your hire last evening. Being both a physical educator and an English teacher was your edge. We feel fortunate that we found someone credentialed in both areas who is also 'young and enthusiastic' as you described yourself." Principal Howie was smiling broadly. He offered to help Carolyn locate an apartment, "since boarding house rates would take a chunk of your paycheck."

Carolyn smiled back with joy and relief, saying "Thank you for your vote of confidence in me. I'll review the contract and let you know in 48 hours. It would be a joy to teach in your new building, and the gym, hockey and softball fields are impressive. Please thank Mrs. Scotton, Mr. Garber, and Miss Parsons for making me feel so at home."

When she pulled into her parents' driveway after a peaceful cruise over the Delaware flatlands, she was amazed that Selbyville School and its people seemed so "right" for her individual talents and interests. The past three days had been postcard perfect. She knew she would accept the position.

CHAPTER THREE

When one conscientiously attempts to effect a constructive deed the universe and its forces join hands to help realize that end.

- Jack Lewis

Jim smiled at the woman who had just sat down near him on the side of the circular fountain in the middle of Washington Square in New York City. "She looks like she loves the water," Jim said, watching the woman's daughter push her sailboat around as she splashed in the fountain.

"Yes, she loves it, and we come here often."

"So do I. I love the trees, the cheap food from the vendors, and the library across the street. What's your daughter's name?"

"It's Ruth Louise, but we call her Ruthie."

"I have a sister named Ruth, and we call her Ruthie too. She's a redhead just like your Ruth. She wrote me yesterday to tell me she is getting married. Life changes quickly."

"Indeed it does."

Jim noticed the pear shaped diamond ring that the woman wore. He judged it to be .85 carat in a yellow gold band with platinum setting. Someone obviously loved her very much. Jim closed his eyes and enjoyed the warm afternoon sun. He needed time to think away from the Manhattan jewelry store. The last three years had been memorable, but he had to admit that he felt like a mouse on a treadmill, always running but going nowhere. When he moved out of his sister Ruth's apartment in Newark, Delaware, he took his total college savings fund and paid his tuition to attend the Peirce School on Pine Street in Philadelphia. The one year training prepared him for an entry level job as a jeweler.

Living in Philadelphia with its trolleys, theaters, and libraries had been stimulating and exciting for a twenty-two year old. Jim had relatives who gave him Sunday dinner and a house to kick back in away from the rented room he shared with another student. Vocational school was not demanding compared to the mathematics and language courses he had taken at Blackstone and Randolph Macon, so he tried to find a weekend job to send some money home. But jobs were scarce as hen's teeth. And, as he saw the lines waiting for the soup kitchens to open, he had felt lucky to be in school with a roof over his head. Most of all, he rejoiced in the theatre. He often waited in line at the Stanley, the Earle, and the Forrest Theaters to pick up discounted seats for previews, or for shows that were about to close.

Today, in fact, he had come to Washington Square because he heard that President Roosevelt's W.P.A. had funded a Federal Theater Project there for summertime park performances. Just beyond the fountain, Jim could see scaffolding that was probably the beginnings of a stage. It was only late March. Jim took a deep breath, stood up, and walked through the park past the bocce courts and the chess tables that were filled with men passing time, just like him. He wondered if he would still be in New York City to enjoy the stage shows when summertime came? Would he be, and should he be, that was the question? He liked his job with Richard E. Weitlich, Inc. on West 46th Street, but he didn't love it. And let's face it, there was a depression on, and people were selling their diamonds more than they were buying them.

As Jim strolled, he felt uncharacteristically depressed. Financially, he was treading water. After two years on the job, his salary didn't go far enough to leave him any savings. New York City prices were higher than in Philadelphia, and he had no family members for support in New York. One day he'd like to be the father of a little girl like the one in the fountain. Jim's stomach growled and his 6 foot 2 inch frame was all skin and bones. He reached in his pocket, and found only 10 cents. Not enough for a decent dinner. How many life plans would it take before he found one that worked?

His sister Ruth's marriage was a bright spot. She was marrying her college sweetheart, the University of Delaware's star running back. But Jim's brother Francis had just been committed to the Home for the Chronically Ill, and none of his brothers had found a real job. His father's railroad hours had been cut back, with the solvency of his pension still unknown.

"Mister, could you tell me where the Library is," a young male voice asked.

"Are you a student?" Jim responded.

"Yes, I began my law studies at N.Y.U. yesterday, and I'm new to the neighborhood."

"The Law Library is just across the square and has a big sign in front of it. You can't miss it."

"Thanks, Mister."

Jim watched the young man head off in the direction Jim had pointed, and he felt more down than ever. It had been seven years since Jim had graduated from high school, and his dream of securing a college education was going nowhere. How he envied the law student who was so much his junior.

Two months later, Jim sat with his eyes closed listening to the clickity clack of the rails and feeling the rhythmic sway of the cars as the train traveled westward. He had tried to sleep for much of the past three days and nights as they traveled through Pennsylvania, Ohio, Indiana, Illinois, Wisconsin, Minnesota, South Dakota and North Dakota. His six foot two frame was crunched like an accordion, and his long legs were screaming to stretch. Eventually

Jim gave up the pretense of sleep and sat upright. His new found friend, Rocco Zarrillo, was snoring slightly beside him. All that Jim knew about Rocco was that he was from New Jersey and that he was a talker. Rocco's stories and laughter had made the train move faster.

It was late on the evening of June 15, 1933, and he was part of the twenty-five member Advance Cadre of the 1224 Company of the Civilian Conservation Corps headed for Camp F-46 in Clarkia, Idaho. Jim already missed the theatre and the excitement of New York City, and he had a definite sense that his days ahead were going to be quite a change of routine.

In the end, the employment choice was made for him. Weitlich Jewelers had apologetically cut his hours in half, citing decreased sales. President Roosevelt had signed the bill authoring the C.C.C., and Jim was enticed to sign up for a six month tour of duty. He was sent to Fort Dupont in Delaware City for orientation and training, and it felt good to return to his home state. He had signed on early, at a time when no one quite knew what the Civilian Conservation Corps meant or what its workers would do. Jim was told that there were not any C.C.C. camps in Delaware, and that he would be sent west. Company 1224 contained 200 men, and he had been selected from several hundred eager candidates who had arrived at Ft. DuPont from New Jersey and Delaware. The selection committee was favorably impressed by his Blackstone Military Academy credentials, even though Jim had read that the C.C.C. would not be under the auspices of the U.S. Military, but rather the Forestry Service and the U.S.

Park Service. At 25 years of age, Jim was considerably older than many of the boys on the train, and few had gone to college as he had done. Jim's maturity, his physical stature, and his well-spoken manner had made him a stand out.

As the train continued its clacking and swaying, Jim thought back on his days as a Bellman at Laurel High and on the Adirondack summer camps he had attended in Plattsburgh, N.Y. His first dream had been to become a military man, a gentleman, and an officer. Now it was too easy to imagine that he was on a path to fulfill a shadow of that dream. Jim glanced down at the government issue uniform he had been given as a Senior Leader. The khaki shirt, pants, and jacket looked a lot like what he had worn at Blackstone. Even though the Fort DuPont officials made it clear that the C.C.C. was not the army, four members of the Advance Cadre were enlisted regular U.S. Army under the direction of Captain Helmer Swenholt. It sure felt to Jim that he had committed to something military in nature.

"Say, what state are we in now?" came Rocco's sleepy voice as he awoke.

"Somewhere in Montana, which is much wider across than Delaware. But I think we are getting close to Missoula because we seemed to have slowed down a bit the last few miles."

"Missoula, Montana' it kinda has a ring to it, doesn't it? I think I'll write a song about Missooooula so we can entertain ourselves because I don't think there's any Broadway in them thar hills."

"Well, it's too dark right now to know what's out there, but I don't see any neon lights," Jim parlayed to keep the conversation going.

"What's a city boy like me doing in a place like this?" Rocco went on.

The train lurched to a sudden halt, and everyone applauded when it was evident that they would disembark. Most of the companies on the packed train were loaded into trucks to begin their journey to Montana work sites. Company 1224, however, was ushered to an antiquated day coach with kerosene lamps, and told that overnight they would be crossing the continental divide, the Bitter Root Range of the Rockies, before arriving at their camp site somewhere in northern Idaho. After an hour, the clickity clack resumed.

At ten o'clock the next morning, Jim and Rocco peered out the window to see the Station sign Clarkia, Idaho, population 59. At last, they were free of the train seats and jubilantly they stretched their gimpy limbs while deeply inhaling the rich Idaho air. They loaded their gear onto the back of a half-ton truck and then climbed up to find a comfortable roost. Jim preferred to stand, holding on to the side railing.

"Captain says its three and a half miles to our camp site," Rocco volunteered. "Hope the rain holds off.

It didn't. As the half ton and two jeeps in their advance party of 25 men lumbered along, the road bed worsened. Black top turned quickly to dirt, and then to ruts and soggy mud as the rain increased. Any semblance of a road disappeared. Twice they climbed down to rock the half ton through the mushy red muck. By noon they arrived, thoroughly drenched, at their work site on Olson Creek in the St. Joe National Forest. Ten years before, the area had been a logging camp, but it had long ago overgrown so that land would need to be cleared to set up tents for the 200 men of the 1224th. Jim had been dozing for days, so he wasn't the least bit sleepy when they all flopped down in sleeping bags after finding the driest possible spot. Tomorrow the real work would begin to establish camp. Jim had never seen trees so big.

Four days later, Jim found sleep to be a speedy and welcome relief for his aching back and muscles. It had been four days of the hardest physical labor Jim had ever done, and he had loved the challenge. With one backho, shovels, picks, and bare hands, they had worked to clear enough land to erect 25 large tents. Even though he wore gloves, Jim's hands burned from pulling out undergrowth and dragging branches to be incinerated. His back ached from slinging the pick and the shovel, but it was a good feeling. At night they slept under a tarp that Rocco had creatively strung between two white pines, just in case of rain. But the night air had been crystal clear so the stars twinkled brilliantly between the swaying Idaho giants. Lying on his back in his sleeping bag, Jim could hear the murmuring creek and the slight sigh of the tall timbers. It was blissfully peaceful, about as far away from Manhattan as one could get.

Today they were expecting the Main Party, 164 strong to arrive from Ft. DuPont under the leadership of 1st Lt. Fremont S. Tandy, 1st Engineers. The increased manpower could finish the job of clearing the camp site and placing floor boards and stoves in the tents. Jim was also looking forward to having a real meal, since the advance party had been eating K rations supplemented with beans and rice. Jim expected better once the mess tent was operational.

I thought we weren't in the Army," Rocco exclaimed loudly as "Reveille" sounded the start of another work day.

"Sure feels like the Army," Jim laughed, hauling his lanky legs up to jog off to the rustic latrine. "Well, I declare!" Rocco shouted after him. "My country needs me, and I've answered the call."

The Main Party was bringing all their forestry equipment, lumber, food, supply tents, medical supplies, recreational items, and the necessary training manuals for forestry conservation. The road from Clarkia to camp was rough, the hills steep, and the curves treacherous. Transporting a large cadre of men in heavily loaded vehicles over infantile roads caused one truck to break down. Those men had to wait with the truck until another could reach the camp, be emptied, return and finally deliver them to their grumbling camp mates who were eager to celebrate the conclusion of their long journey west.

Overnight the camp became a beehive of activity. Morale improved each day as tents capable of housing 8 men were erected and army cots unpacked to support the sleeping bags. Each man got an army blanket, towel, washcloth, and toilet articles. Because he was a reader, Jim knew that the district included 45 Civilian Conservation Corps Camps in northern Idaho, western Montana, and eastern Washington. While some local forestry personnel had been recruited at each site, the majority of enrollees came all the way from New York, New Jersey, and Delaware. Jim felt proud that his country had been able, in the short span of seven weeks, to organize such a mammoth undertaking. Their Camp F-46 in northern Idaho was just one of 1,315 C.C.C. camps across the country established to date, with more planned. The logistics of it all amazed Jim, and instilled in him a greater reverence for the Quartermaster Corps of the U.S. Army.

Every man was expected to learn the basics of forestry conservation, even though twenty percent of their cadre was assigned to cook, purchase supplies, and build their mess hall, kitchen, and shower room. Jim and Rocco listened as Forestry Servicemen explained the fundamentals of blister rust control. Blister rust is a destructive spore disease which cannot attack from pine to pine, but must be carried to the white pine by the host plants, wild currant and goose-berry bushes. Their mission was to eradicate the carrier plants by spraying those on the mountain sides and hand pulling those on the creek banks. Since most of the men of F-46 were city boys who didn't know a wild currant or goose-berry bush from poison sumac, training was mandatory for all.

Rocco was the first to volunteer to strap the spray tank on his back and threaten everyone with the insecticide wand. "I'm a Jersey boy who can goose those wild berries; just let me at em!" Rocco dramatized. For several days, the cadre combed the hills and creek beds under supervision, identifying the carrier plants and learning how to mix the proper levels of DDT with water. But before long, they were on their own, "talking blister rust" like forest rangers.

In camp, floor boards were laid in each tent which greatly improved warmth, cleanliness, and morale. Then construction began on the mess hall, kitchen, and bath facilities. Thirteen local men, most of them carpenters, had been newly enrolled from surrounding towns, bringing the unit strength up to 213. As the days and nights passed, friendships formed and work assignments solidified. Jim and Rocco seemed to complement each other's skills, so they continued to be together much of each day. Jim took the lead, but Rocco got things done quickly, sometimes ahead of himself. Jim was seven years older, had completed 1½ years of college, and was a thinker who was cautious with his words. He understood military protocol and was highly organized. He also was a certified jeweler, which had no application in the forests of Coeur D'Alene. Rocco was barely 18, fresh out of high school, and utterly street smart, which did have some use, even in the wilderness. Rocco could fix any piece of equipment that had an ailment. He could size up any situation that involved people, and come up with a quip that defused the situation, usually with good humor. Like the first day on the train, Jim enjoyed Rocco's company because he was just fun to be around.

Today Jim was using his height and army issued field glasses to mark boundaries for work sectors. "To the left, watch the drop," Jim shouted, "that looks good, paint it!" A blob of white paint was plastered on the tree trunk, rock, or bush to mark the boundary of the work area. By marking sectors, the men could return later to pull up the carrier bushes once they withered, and to re-spray where necessary. Each hillside area was numbered on a master map in Capt. Swenholt's tent , and he reported weekly on the unit's progress to his superiors at district headquarters at Ft. George Wright in Spokane, Washington, about 100 miles from Camp F-46.

"It's busier than the Atlantic City boardwalk on the Fourth of July, Rocco mused as he charged up the hill beside Jim. Laughing, Jim had to agree. Gazing across the sloping terrain, Jim could see boys swarming the slope, waving their wands, and attacking the hosts. It was only ten a.m., but already they had filled one half ton with brush. Both men were covered with dust since there had been no rain, except for the downpour on the night the advance party arrived. Blister rust work was truly monotonous and called for resiliency of effort. Every foot of ground was checked and re-checked to kill every possible disease carrier. It was tedious, and at times back breaking work, as some of the bigger bushes refused to let go of the Idaho soil. Jim's group had designated "George the Giant" as their hit man for stubborn roots. At 275 lbs. with biceps and thighs like a wrestler, George could pull anything up. On those rare times when he couldn't, the men formed a tug of war to dislodge the root ball. One day was very much like the next, and the men kept their sanity with games and chatter led by Rocco, and the sense of accomplishment in knowing that their work was protecting the "fat of the land."

It didn't take long for Jim to realize that the white pine tree was the economic backbone of the whole Northwest. People in the neighboring towns of St. Maries, Bevill, Moscow, Clarkia, and further away in Spokane, were quick to praise the work of the C.C.C. to protect the pines from disease, as well as from forest fires. Several of the local experienced carpenters had told Jim about the devastating fires of 1910 which killed 100 people and destroyed thousands of acres of virgin timber. Without the white pine, most of the local businesses would collapse. Jim found comfort in knowing that his daily labor was making a difference.

CHAPTER FOUR

The farm is the most elemental of industries. The design of the farm has tamed soil and beast to serve the farmer. Farmer, beast of burden, and the soil, form a trinity wherein each part is necessary to the whole.

- Jack Lewis

"I found the six newborns when I dashed out in the storm to close the barn door," Cora chatted. "Hadn't even noticed this time that she was in a family way."

Carolyn assessed that Cora Quillen was jovial, smart, and not one to suffer fools gladly. Her dinner table was full of turkey, cornbread stuffing, mashed potatoes, gravy, yeast rolls, and an assortment of vegetables. The warm food tasted comforting after the long drive Carolyn made in the driving rain, which had never eased all the way from Swarthmore to Selbyville.

Everyone was getting to know each other. It was a bit awkward, but exhilarating. George and Cora Quillen were 'young marrieds' in Cora speak, who farmed a considerable tract of land outside of town. On Principal Howie's recommendation, Carolyn agreed over the phone to rent a room in their second floor apartment, which, like the high school, had just been finished. She would have her own bedroom, and share a bath and living-kitchen area with another woman. Principal Howie assured her that the apartment had indoor plumbing, and he bragged that it also had a newfangled air conditioning unit for the late summer days ahead. Carolyn signed the lease for the month of August and thereafter for eleven months. Anxious to begin her new life, she arrived August 3rd with hopes of arranging several field hockey practice sessions before Labor Day.

"Pass the collards, if you don't mind," George requested. He appeared to be a man of few words, very tall and slim in stature, with a no nonsense demeanor like Cora, only more serious. Cora was giggling as she talked a mile a minute. Carolyn had to concentrate to catch all the words of the story Cora was telling about their barnyard cat that had just given birth that afternoon to six kittens between the claps of thunder and flashes of lightning.

Odette Wright, Carolyn's roommate, was seated across the table from her. She appeared to be several years older than Carolyn, and she had lovely creamy skin that Carolyn surmised was smoothly tanned from time in the Atlantic Ocean. Odette had dark, sparkling eyes, that absorbed the whole room and seemed to observe everything at once. Her voice was soft and calm, the opposite of Cora's quick cadence. Odette was shorter than Carolyn, but then most women were shorter than Carolyn. Carolyn had been told that her roommate was studying to be a teacher, and that she helped the Quillens with farm chores in turn for a reduction in her rent.

Dessert was the most scrumptious peach pie Carolyn had ever tasted. Nothing she had eaten in Europe or at the Inglenuk could even come close. "Just picked these peaches this morning at Bennett's Orchard," Cora shared. "These are the White Lady variety that have just ripened, and I think they make the best pies." Carolyn made a mental note to try to obtain Cora's pie crust recipe as Cora made it clear "that dinner would be served at the dining room table each evening, and breakfast was 'serve yourself', except for Sunday morning when they would meet early for a special breakfast before church." Lunch, of course, would be at school.

It was still raining and pitch dark when Carolyn dragged her suitcase up the steps to her new apartment. Her bedroom was large and contained a single bed, one chest of drawers with a mirror, and a closet. There was plenty of space for a desk, lamp, and lounge chair, all which Carolyn planned to purchase locally. There was no bedroom window, but the living area between the two bedrooms had a large window over a sink set in a kitchen type counter. The one bathroom, located off the living room, had a sink, toilet, and a shower, but no tub. All in all, it was quite satisfactory.

Carolyn unpacked only the essentials, and after exchanging pleasantries with Odette, made up her bed and gleefully crawled under the covers. It had been a long, eventful, day, her first as a resident of Sussex County, Delaware.

Daylight brought bright sunlight to the Quillen farm, but Carolyn slept like a rock in her very dark windowless bedroom. When she finally arose, she was annoyed at herself for sleeping until 9 a.m. She had intended to rise early and take a walk around the farm before heading into town. Then she planned to unpack the boxes of books in the trunk of her Buick and begin to arrange her homeroom. Stepping out into the common space on the way to the bathroom, Carolyn could see that Odette's bedroom door was open and she was gone. After dressing in her favorite sweater, saddle shoes and slacks, Carolyn grabbed her car keys and hurried down the steps.

At the foot of the steps she came to an abrupt halt. Her mouth fell open in amazement, but no words emerged. Before her was a blanket of white fluff as far as she could see. The cotton puffs were moving, twittering like, going nowhere but constantly in motion. They were chicks, baby chickens, and there were thousands of them! Carolyn collapsed on the bottom step and sat mesmerized by the high pitched chirps of the little white critters. On closer inspection, the chicks were jostling around feeder jars of water and pushing each other toward long metal troughs of what looked like cornmeal. The whole ground floor of her apartment was alive with squeaky fluff that was apparently very hungry. For heaven's sake, how had she missed this last night?

"Odette!" Carolyn boomed out as she headed down the corridor in the center of the exceptionally long space. She could see a partially open door at the very end of the house, but the exit had to be several hundred feet from where she was standing. "Odette, are you there?" No answer. The only sound was the chirping of an ocean of white chicken fluff.

When she finally located her inside a second chicken house, Odette had a big grin on her face and a huge sack of cornmeal in both hands. "How are you this fine morning?" Odette exclaimed as she set the big burlap bag down by her feet. For once, Carolyn couldn't think of anything appropriate to say. Odette continued, "We had no idea the biddies were coming this morning; we expected them next week. The trucks arrived at 5:30 a.m. because things go better in the dark with chickens. I hope the noise didn't disturb you."

"No, I had absolutely no idea. How many of them are there?

"Twelve thousand, give or take a few. I was going to give you a crash course tonight in the care and feeding of Rhode Island Reds. Aren't they enchanting creatures?" Odette said slowly, as if to test Carolyn's reaction.

"Yes, I'd appreciate your short course on what to expect the next month or so. How long does it take before you sell them? You couldn't possibly eat them all," Carolyn snipped, making a half-hearted attempt at humor.

"Twelve weeks, if things go well," Odette smiled.

They agreed to talk again after dinner, and Carolyn headed for her car, feeling more than a little bit hoodwinked.

When Carolyn returned to the Quillen farm mid-afternoon, she was tired but exhilarated from setting up her classroom. She had reveled in unlimited quiet time to sit at her desk in room 9B, unpack her boxes of English books and teaching references, and rearrange her students' desks. In the center of her desk, she found the teacher's copy of the newly selected ninth grade English text, *English Essentials,* which she tucked into her bag to study thoroughly at her apartment.

At the foot of the apartment steps, Carolyn paused once again to gaze the length of the chicken house. The sight still amazed her. Thousands of twittering fluff balls. All chirping. She noticed that one little chick, or peep, as Odette called it, had wandered away from the others. He looked lost but adventuresome, a feeling she could relate to. She bent over and scooped up the soft lump of fluff to her chest. Oh, he was so cute! The biddie was trembling, but Carolyn didn't think it was fear as much as just his nature. She returned him to the mass of peeping chicks that were huddled together, then quickly scooped him up again. Then she bent down and picked up a piece of red twine that she guessed had fallen to the floor from a feed bag. Gently she tied the twine around the right leg of the little critter. There now, she might be able to find him tomorrow so they could continue to get to know each other.

Quillen's Farm
RD #2
Selbyville, Delaware

Dear Virginia,

I've gone to the birds, literally! Never in my wildest dreams could I have imagined I'd be living in a chicken house apartment over thousands of baby birds. Words cannot describe the sight. Needless to say, I'm still adjusting to the situation, but then, I recall that I wanted an unscripted scenario. (I can just hear your voice telling me that now.) Miss you already.

George and Cora Quillen, the owners of the farm where I live, have been warm and gracious to me. My roommate, Odette Wright is studying to be a teacher. She seems nice enough, but we haven't had much time to talk because she has 12,000 biddies to care for at the moment. Odette also works another job on weekends and somehow finds time for her courses at Delaware State College.

I'll be expecting a letter from you now that you have my address. Do write soon to tell me about Pottstown High and your living accommodations. Do you like your colleagues? Are you teaching any summer school sessions prior to the beginning of fall classes? I haven't

*met any of my students yet, but will at my first hockey
meeting next week.*

*Must run. Will write again soon.
As ever, Carolyn*

Carolyn was finally getting the short course on Rhode Island Reds, and Odette was saying, "We have to keep them warm right now until they grow a bit. My job is to keep coal in the brooder stoves, water in the fountains, and mash in the troughs. The biddies eat a lot and they drink even more."

"Fountains? Do you mean the round ceramic containers with a dish of water under them?" Carolyn asked.

"Yes, we call them fountains and they have to be washed out and refilled daily. Sometimes we add nutrients to the water to protect against disease."

"I hadn't noticed the stoves. But I guess that explains why the chicken house is always slightly warm, even at night, Carolyn surmised.

"Well, it's a much easier job in summer than in December, but I keep a close eye on the temperature even now because they are small. And I always stoke up the stoves before bedtime, and then first thing in the morning, if it's chilly. Cold and dampness will kill off biddies quicker than a fox."

"You sure know a lot about chickens, Odette."

"Well I was taught by the best. 'The Lady' taught me everything I know."

"Who?"

"The Lady, Mrs. Cecile Steele. She was the first person to figure out that raising broilers was a lot more profitable than having layers. In 1923, she ordered 50 chicks to restock her laying hens, and instead she was sent 500. She put them in the large crate her piano had been shipped in, and 8 weeks later she sold the 387 still alive for a huge profit. The next year she ordered 1,000 chicks and the following year 10,000, after her husband built her some chicken houses. My people and the Lady's family go way back. My father helped Wilmer Steele build Cecile's first broiler houses. I grew up feeding Cecile's chicks."

"No wonder the Quillens want you here to get their new poultry operation off the ground. I can see that it comes second nature to you, and that you love it, Odette."

"It's in my blood, Carolyn, but that doesn't make it any less back breaking. Hauling 100 pound feed bags and shoveling coal will work for me now, but I better get a college education so I can teach one day. Tell me about your job at Selbyville High School."

Carolyn explained her split responsibilities as a ninth grade English teacher, and as teacher of ninth through twelve grade girls' physical education. She explained that she would need to stay after school to coach field hockey in the fall, basketball in the winter, and softball in the spring.

"I'd give anything to be where you are now, Carolyn. I'm just beginning my fundamentals of education classes, so my dream of teaching fourth grade is a long way off."

"Odette, isn't Delaware State College in Dover? As I recall from my drive south, that's an hour and a half from here.

"Yes, I get up before dawn on my two class days to allow time for the drive, after I feed the chickens of course. I bike to town and catch a ride on the mail truck since it makes a collection stop at the College before heading to Wilmington. Usually I can bum a ride home with another student. If not, I walk to Cheswold where my Uncle lives. He comes south every morning, very early, to work the menhaden boats out of Lewes. He's kind enough to swing south to get me to the Quillen's. It he's running late, he drops me at my cousin Mabel's in Sandtown and she drives me to Selbyville."

"Whew! What a routine, Carolyn exclaimed, realizing for the first time that Odette did not own a car.

"Well, it's only two days a week, since that is all I can pay for right now. Sometimes I can catch a snooze in the mail truck, if I'm not studying, and its peaceful at my Uncle's until we get up to leave at 2:30 a.m."

"Odette, I'd be very happy to drive you to town so you can forgo the bicycle. You know I go early every weekday."

"Thanks, that would be wonderful."

Before retiring for the night, Odette and Carolyn shared that they both had brothers. Odette's was five years older and his name was Leonard. He had his own fishing boat and commercially fished in winter, and Captained fishing charters during the summer.

Carolyn's brother, Charles, was a sophomore in high school.

The sheets felt blissful after Carolyn had a warm shower and reflected on her first day in her classroom. She had learned much from the evening chat with Odette, and she had newfound respect for the resiliency of her roommate. She liked how things were unfolding, chickens and all.

Two weeks passed, and Carolyn found herself enjoying their dinnertime discussions, or perhaps it was Cora's cooking. They had just devoured chicken and dumplings, peas, sliced tomatoes, buttermilk biscuits, and peach pie. Carolyn couldn't seem to get enough of the hearty fare which tasted so fresh and light, even though it surely would begin to show soon on her tall, slim, figure. Carolyn got plenty of exercise teaching her physical education classes and running up and down the hockey field, but she doubted that would balance out Cora's wonderful calories.

"What do you mean Tioga Feed Company raised the rate?" Cora quizzed Odette over the last of the pie.

"Jimmy says they have to charge five cents more because Jack Hill raised his bag price. I can see if Red Comb Feed in Ocean View or Murray Feed in Frankford will give us a better price. Or do you want to stay with Tioga? They have always given me great service and no fillers in the mash, Odette reported."

"Why don't you check out the other," George spoke up, "and let Cora make the decision."

"How are the biddies doing? Let's see, we've had them fifteen days, and it appears all is well," Cora continued. "Are you happy with things?"

"Very satisfied. We've only lost two, and that was from transport trauma. The weather temperature has been cool for August, so no chance of heat pile up or smothering. They are eating well and I can see the first signs that their plumage is coming on," Odette summarized.

"Wonderful. Let's pray the good Lord that we get a strong bid come October. It would be nice to help pay off the loan on our expanded operation," Cora said wistfully.

"Carolyn," Cora asked, "would you like to ride Saturday afternoon to Camp Meeting with George and me? You will probably see some of your students there, and the experience might help you get to know them better. We aren't spending the night, just having dinner there, and coming home after the evening service."

"Sure, I'd love to go. Why don't I drive since putting three adults in the cab of your truck is too cozy."

"Odette, would you like to come with us?" Carolyn asked.

"No thanks, my people have different practices, and I really need to study."

Quillen's Farm
RD#2
Selbyville, Delaware

Dear Ginny,

Thanks for your letter and all the Pottstown High news. I'm impressed by the credentials of some of your colleagues and by the reasonable class sizes. You are fortunate to teach in such a rich learning environment and be close to Bob to boot. Let me know when he pops the question. Now that you both have your college degrees and jobs, I'm sure he will be asking you to marry him, as soon as he feels financially able.

My roomie and I are getting along smashingly well. Odette is a hard working poultry consultant who is studying to become an elementary teacher. She has a great smile and sense of humor, and she is even tempered and mature like you, (but I never said that). She has made reference to "my people," and I'm going to get up my nerve soon to ask her what she means.

On Saturday, I had quite an experience. I went to Carey's Camp with Cora and George. It's a religious event that is worship, evangelism, recreation, and community celebration, all in one. Many of the hymns I had not sung before, but everyone knew them by heart and sang with such gusto. At 5:30 the covered pavilion where we had been singing was instantly filled with casseroles and pies of all description. People were politely pushing to get a piece of Cora's peach pie. The children finished their meals quickly and the boys began a baseball game, while most of the girls played jacks, tag and hide and seek.

At 7:00 the pavilion became a "tabernacle" for

worship by adding more chairs and placing a raised platform at one end. A Methodist minister led the service, but Cora told me there were Baptists, Lutherans, and Pentecostals there too. The service was nothing like we are used to at Swarthmore Presbyterian. There was a lot of shouting, even when they prayed. They sang and they prayed with such fervor that God must have surely been listening. As the songs echoed in the warm evening air, I felt close to the spirit myself.

But the best part was the featured speaker. He was a young Methodist minister visiting from West Virginia, and oh, did he get my attention! Ginny, he had a voice like an angel, and a keen mind as well. Not to mention he was tall, blue eyed, and so handsome. He spoke about waiting on the Lord through tough times. I think his message taken from David's Twenty-Seventh Psalm, "Wait for the Lord; be strong and take heart and wait for the Lord," had special meaning, given the depression and last summer's drought that people still talk about. I know it was the best sermon I have heard, ever. After the service, I had to ask someone the young Reverend's name since there was no written program to refer to. I was told it was "Al Taylor" and that he was "spoken for," whatever that means in these parts.

I know I'm going on about Carey's Camp, but just one more amazing fact. Remember the big doll houses we used to play with in my attic? You know how they had some rooms with open fronts? Well, they have bigger versions of our doll houses here. They call them *"tents" even though they are cottages that sit side by side in a huge circle all around the Tabernacle. Each tent is a story and a half with the ground level open, like our doll houses. Families who own "tents" come and stay for a couple of weeks, so it truly is like a camp. I imagine it requires some social status to secure one of the cottages.*

Keep the letters coming, and I promise to do the same. Just seeing your handwriting makes me smile.

Best ever,
Carolyn

CHAPTER FIVE

Paintings have invariably a prelude of dread and abandonment. Yet simultaneous with this dread is the strong resolution to produce something. The triumph of this resolution over the feeling of dread measures the worth of the result.

- Jack Lewis

Jim edged closer to the light of the campfire to read the letter from home. His father had written to thank him for the first payment he had received for Jim's C.C.C. work. The Kelleys had been sent a check for $25, all but $5 of Jim's first month's earnings, and his parents were so elated that the letter itemized where every penny would be spent. At home, things were as well as could be expected, but far from happy. His father was still working a part-time schedule, and the inquiry into the solvency of his Pennsylvania Railroad pension was still unanswered. Jim's brother, Charles, had decided to join the Navy and would be off to basic training by the end of the month.

Rocco was sprawled out beside Jim around the roaring fire. "What's the feature entertainment for the evening?" Rocco quipped. "Cotton Club Jazz? Broadway dancers? Las Vegas show girls?"

"Just our social highlight of the week, our own Lt. Tom Tandy reciting another installment in 'The History of West Point', Jim retorted, amazed that he was as interested as he was in the Lieutenant's oration. Jim and Rocco's corner of the St. Joe's National Forest was a long way from the footlights of Philadelphia and New York City, and Rocco had been absolutely right to predict on the train that there would be "no Broadway in them thar hills."

"Let's get on with the story-telling and singing, anything but this," Rocco grumbled. Soon Rocco got his wish when enrollee Ralph Sampson of Stockley, Delaware, masterfully blew his mouth organ, to render his Idaho version of the familiar song, "Bury Me Not on the Lone Prairie." Then some of the New York boys wrote a parody on "Shuffle Off To Buffalo," and sang in unison with much gusto:

> Oh we loved our vaccinations
> But those damned inoculations
> Darn near laid us low-O-O-O
> And now we've got to hustle to
> Shuffle off to Idaho!

It was corny, but it was the only show in town, and

groups of men competed to be designated the best, or the worst, act of the night. Late in the evening, someone would invariably sound out the C.C.C. battle cry, "We can take it!" and all would join in the rousing chant that echoed through the tall trees, "We can take it! We can take it!"

Saturday was a shortened work day for cleaning equipment, repairing and refilling spray cans, cleaning uniforms, and restocking supplies. Come afternoon, men were mountain hiking, hitching rides to town, or playing baseball against neighboring C.C.C. camps on the branches of Mary Creek. By the end of their first month, most men had gained considerable weight and felt stronger than ever. The crystal clear Idaho air was partly responsible, but truth be known, most of the men had arrived undernourished at Ft. DuPont and the other C.C.C. training camps. At enrollment, they were hungry young men, who caused the Quartermaster Corps to increase its daily mess rations during the first two months of operation. After a few months, the regular food rations proved adequate. Government issue breakfast included oatmeal, fresh milk, fried eggs, and bacon, hashed brown potatoes, bread, butter and coffee. Lunch might be roast pork and gravy, baked or creamed potatoes, peas, cabbage or slaw, rice pudding, bread butter and coffee. Dinner could include braised ribs of beef, mashed potatoes and gravy, creamed string beans, fresh fruit, salad, apple pie, bread and butter, hot cocoa and coffee. Jim and Rocco ate ravenously at first, not quite believing their good fortune. It was such a luxury not to have to worry about food and shelter. Jim, who had arrived gaunt and straggly, immediately put on fifteen pounds, in spite of the rigorous physical activity.

By mid-summer the drought had become an issue. No substantial rain had fallen since their June arrival, and the Forestry Service had issued a high fire alert. Large water buckets were filled and placed near the Friday night camp fire. Two nearby fire towers were manned around the clock to search for smoke or other fire hazards, while routine patrols canvased the hillsides. The men were taught how to operate a tanker truck of water that had recently been allocated to Camp F-46. Looking at the sheer size of the tall pines, Jim doubted that the tanker would have more than a tea cup impact on any raging inferno, but he thought it might give his unit time to make an escape to safety.

"Is that another poem you are writing for Lady Elaine?" Jim teased Rocco.   Rocco ignored him and kept writing by the light of the kerosene lamp in their tent that they shared with six other men. After dinner, there was time to read or talk, and Jim liked talking to no one better than Rocco. He might frequently play the clown, but Jim found Rocco to be quite the gentleman. Rocco's real name was Nicholas, and it seemed his family called him Nick. As a Jersey boy, Rocco hid his sensitive side, but to Jim he talked about his girlfriend Elaine who worked as a secretary in Jersey City. Rocco's earnings were being sent to his parents, but he had asked them, if they could, to give Elaine one or two dollars each week. Rocco wrote love poems and sent them to Elaine, causing Jim to smile as he remembered the poems he had hidden from his brothers. Jim's handwriting was absolutely beautiful, like the sample from a Palmer Method penmanship sheet. Rocco's handwriting looked like hen scratching, and Jim noted some errors in grammar. But then Rocco didn't really need to write longhand because he was the fastest typist Jim had ever seen. Quite unexpectedly, Jim had gone to the equipment tent one Saturday afternoon looking for a baseball glove, and there he had discovered Rocco flying away on the camp's third typewriter that had been discarded because of a faulty key. Rocco, of course, had fixed the mechanical mishap in no time, and was pounding out a love letter at an amazing rate.

"Is that skill noted in your records file?" Jim casually asked, trying not to look surprised.

"Yes, of course, but they never ask you to do something you're qualified for."

"How true," Jim smiled. What was a jeweler like himself, who wanted nothing more than to finish college, doing fighting blister rust in Idaho?

In time, Jim's equipment room revelation cemented a working relationship between Rocco and Jim that would last several years. Jim could write, and Rocco could type. They teamed up to begin documenting camp activities. What at first was a hobby to kill time, soon became a second job as their printed editions received rave reviews. After all, they were the only local press, and everyone liked to read about themselves.

On July 22, Jim was appointed Official Camp Reporter for the *C.C.C. News*, which was printed in Spokane. Headquarters decided to publish a weekly newspaper documenting corps accomplishments and camp life. Senior Leader James A. Kelley, who had just been elevated to First Sergeant, was the natural choice of Captain Swenholt at Camp F-46. Thus Jim and Rocco were sanctioned to make the world aware of all the good and crazy things that were happening on Olsen Creek. Weekly editions of the *C.C.C. News* raised esprit de corps and promoted healthy competition among the twelve camps in St. Joes Forest. One of its earliest installments announced the new official motto of the Civilian Conservation Corps, "We Can Take It!" which had become a favorite chant at F-46 Friday night bonfires. For Jim and Rocco, the news assignment was a labor of love that made the days fly by faster for both of them.

In late August Jim and Rocco were waiting in the line for the showers. Most men liked to get cleaned up before heading into the chow line for dinner, and late afternoon was a popular time in the wash house. Electric lines had not reached their camp site, so daylight made it easier to scrub up clean. Their water supply was spring water from the west fork of Olsen Creek, and it was heated in the shower area by wood and coal, just like the stove pipe heater in their tent.

"I saw the Captain take a telegram from the Western Union courier out to St. Marie's an hour ago," Rocco whispered to the man in front of him. "My guess is that our skipper is asking his superiors what will happen to us come October." The rumors had already started to fly. Would the C.C.C. continue and who would choose to re-enroll? If it continued, would they work here or somewhere else? Would the unit stay together or be scattered? Two of their regular army officers had recently been transferred to other companies in Montana. What did that mean for the future of F-46? Would they ever get out of this increasingly colder place? By God's grace, they had survived the hottest parts of the rainless summer, with no forest fires, and now, with the cooling days and downright cold nights, Jim could sense the rainy season approaching. It could get soggy before the frost set in. Jim was sure he wouldn't want to be in the St. Joe's Forest in December.

September was decision month. Enrollees had to declare re-enrollment or release. It was their choice, but it was not an easy one since second termers were given no information on their future assignments. Most men of the F-46 were convinced that their camp could not continue to function during the Idaho winter, and having completed their blister rust mission, there was little to do anyway. The fall rains and winter snows that were sure to follow would make forest fires highly unlikely. It was a foregone conclusion that they would be moving somewhere.

By the time the orders arrived, 44 members had signified their desire to re-enroll. Jim and Rocco were among them. All but 27 men were being sent back to Camp Dix, N.J. for discharge or reassignment. 27 of the re-enrollees had been surprisingly assigned to C.C.C. Headquarters at Ft. Lewis, Washington, 400 miles away on the Pacific coast. They left a day ahead of the main contingent, putting a damper on the last camp bonfire. That night the men sang "Shuffle Off To Idaho" one last time, but with a new melancholy. Weenies were roasted, speeches were made, but the gusto was lacking. Although most of the boys were glad to be going home, very few of them liked the idea of leaving the tall pines, the delightful little creek, and the rugged hills which were so different from the east coast flatlands.

Jim and Rocco were both selected to stay, with 15 others, for one more week of hard work. All government property had to be checked and packed for the return train ride home. The camp was being completely evacuated, with the 9 local experienced woodsmen transferred to another Clarkia camp as soon as the post-camp clean-up was finished. Finally, on Sunday, October 15, 1933, Capt. Swenholt, Lt. McTernan, Jim, Rocco, and two other enlisted men, boarded the train at Clarkia, made a stop at St. Maries, and then headed east for New Jersey.

Rocco was elated that he was going home. Elaine was going to meet him at Camp Dix and he had her telegram in his pocket confirming that she had received his wire. As the train rails clacked in his ear, Jim could feel the uneasiness and sense of dread seep into his soul again. He wondered what hand life would deal him next? College didn't seem to be in the cards.

In Chicago, the train made a stop and Jim and Rocco had a few hours to visit the Century of Progress World's Fair. It was their first venture into city life in four months, and it seemed strange to hear so many sounds and see so many people at once. And where were the trees? Jim ran between exhibit halls to absorb as much as he could in five hours. It was quite eye opening for an inquisitive young man from Delmar, Delaware to glimpse the world's future in aviation, automobiles, electricity, and something called natural gas. Jim hadn't felt so alive since his Randolph Macon days of independent study in the campus library.

They arrived in Camp Dix on October 19, train weary, but glad to be "home." Elaine was there to meet Rocco and he promptly got permission to take a three day leave. Jim did his duty as a member of the unloading crew and then tried to get comfortable on post with no assigned quarters and no orders to ease his mind. Nearly two weeks passed before he learned that the remnant of the 1224th Company would be sent to Lewes, Delaware. Now Jim was the one who would be going home.

Left Section of Group Photo: Men of Civilian Conservation Corps Camp F-46, on Olsen Creek, Coeur D'Alene National Forest, Idaho, from Jim Kelley's scrapbook with permission from the U. S. National Archives and Records Administration.

Center Left Section of Group Photo: Men of Civilian Conservation Corps Camp F-46 from Jim Kelley's scrapbook with permission from the U. S. National Archives and Records Administration.

Center Right Section of Group Photo: Jim Kelley is pictured center right, fourth row, in back of man with crossed arms in dark jacket, who is believed to be "Rocco" Nick Zarrillo. From Jim Kelley's scrapbook with permission from the U. S. National Archives and Records Administration.

Right Section of Group Photo: From Jim Kelley's scrapbook with permission from the U. S. National Archives and Records Administration.

CHAPTER SIX

There is a challenge in this race
of people who sing and dance
even in greatest times of stress.
- Jack Lewis

"I'm sorry that hockey practice ran late. You shouldn't have held up supper for me," Carolyn apologized as she hurried to take her seat across from Odette.

"We understand, honey. In heat like this, no one feels like eating anything until the sun sets and it begins to cool off," Cora said, as she passed the iced tea. "Sure must have been a chicken choker on the hockey field today."

"It was a scorcher. I had to make sure they all drank enough water, and I cut out the extra laps. We have our first scrimmage tomorrow against Laurel and then our first game next week against Georgetown. Sure hope it cools off my then."

"How's the team look?"

"Well, Cora, it's hard for me to judge until I see the competition. But my girls are so attentive and eager to learn. I wish some of them had as much concentration in English class as they do on the hockey field."

"Pass the applesauce, if you don't mind," came George's always polite and succinct request.

Carolyn's day had been focused on topic sentences and gym suits. Her two ninth grade English classes had struggled to write more paragraphs than she wanted to grade, and she had to have a talk with three gym girls who claimed they couldn't afford to buy the required gym suits and sneakers. She'd check with the school nurse in the morning because Nurse Palmer seemed to know the most about each student's home situation.

Odette was unusually quiet at dinner, and Carolyn noticed that she looked preoccupied. After heading up the apartment steps together, Carolyn went into her bedroom to relax, shower, and grade paragraphs so tomorrow's class could be more instructive. Odette excused herself, saying she was going downstairs to check on the brood.

About nine o'clock, Carolyn took a break in grading papers and fixed a glass of iced tea. As she sat at their utility table, she could hear the apartment window air conditioner grinding away. She also noticed that the window curtain was made out of a chicken feed bag. It was cotton burlap material, but quite colorful with a lovely flowered pattern. Probably Cora's creative handiwork.

Carolyn stood and stretched her lanky legs. She was curious about why Odette was gone so long, but she wasn't thrilled about heading downstairs to look for her. In the heat, the chicken house was taking on an ammonia smell. Now she understood why her bedroom had no window, and why Principal Howie had highlighted "the new-fangled air conditioning unit." What a difference the small unit affixed to their kitchen window made! It allowed them to keep their apartment window closed to the heat, farm noises, and the ever-increasing smells of summer. Carolyn was amazed that she had discovered this invention in southern Delaware, far from suburban Philadelphia modernity. "I think you should buy a unit for your bedroom," she had written her parents. "An old farm boy like me likes to sleep with the bedroom windows open," was her father's flat refusal to look into the purchase.

In the usual spot at the foot of the steps, Carolyn paused. It was becoming a habit. She stood quiet as a cornstalk and watched as Odette did a slow run through the chicken house, swerving from side to side to force the birds to scuttle away. It was somewhat of a song and dance because Odette purred sweetly as she jogged, "move you sweet darlings; hustle up you biddies; skedaddle you little critters!" Odette waved her arms as she danced and hopped. The girl had rhythm and she was totally engrossed in her music.

As soon as Odette saw Carolyn, she stopped and smiled.

"You have a lovely voice," Carolyn complimented.

"Thanks. My people love to sing and dance."

Carolyn was about to ask Odette what she meant by "my people" when Odette said she was extremely worried about the chicks.

"I thought things were going well, as you told Cora last week," Carolyn responded.

"In chicken time, a week is an ice age. Things can change quickly. I found three birds dead this evening."

It was then that Carolyn noticed the pile of feathers near the doorway. "What do you do with the carcasses? Is that the right term?"

"I'll bury two of them at the back of the property, and one I'll take to the state lab in Dover for testing. They might help me know why they died. I'm sure it's not the heat, even though I've been running like a mad woman to counter its effects. It just hasn't been hot long enough to make them die."

"Is there anything I can do to help?" Carolyn offered.

"Thanks, but I just finished refilling all of the fountains.   With the heat, the birds require more water and a little less feed. I'm going to make a run through the last house, and then we can talk upstairs," Odette said, as she zig-zagged down the aisle toward the second chicken house, still waving her arms and singing.

"OK. See you in a few," Carolyn shouted.

Carolyn turned to bolt up the steps, and then she stopped, turned and walked over to the heap of the three dead chickens. They were limp and pitiful looking, but she forced herself to examine all their legs. None had a red string tied to it.

Two days later, Carolyn came down the steps to find the chicken house full of visitors. From the last step, she watched in amazement as the vaccinating crew worked like a surgical team huddled in an operating room. Two women sat on folding chairs, their knees touching, beside two other women who sat, knees meeting. On each end of the group of four chairs were "catchers" and "passers." With 'grab the last biscuit speed', the chicken was snatched and then passed to three of the seated women, who like lightning, flipped the bird over so its rear end was exposed. The forth woman, who held a small bottle filled with fluid used a brush to swipe the three exposed rear ends. Swish, swish, swish! It was all done in an instant, and the three chickens were gently slung to the side so they scattered away across the chicken house floor.

Carolyn stood still, taking in the drill over and over. Grab, snatch, flip, swish, release! One, two, three, four, five! And then grab again. With incredible speed and efficiency, the process continued while the crew carried on intermittent conversation. Carolyn noticed that one of the passers was a girl about 14 years old who looked familiar. Perhaps she had seen the perky teen at the intramural Play Day the Selbyville High girls organized for the middle school girls. Carolyn wondered if there were child labor laws in Sussex County like there had been at the suburban Philadelphia community centers. Or perhaps the young girl, who had just been called "Ruthie," *was* being paid. Who would do this hot, sweaty, dusty work from sun up to sunset without some payback? Vaccinating 12.000 chicks might even take a second day to complete. Certainly the crew had arrived early because they had already vaccinated half the pullets in the first room of the chicken house. Grab, snatch, flip, swish, release! It was mesmerizing.

As she headed for her car, Carolyn made a mental note to ask Odette for what disease the chickens were being vaccinated. Odette must have been worried to hire that many people and inoculate every bird on the Quillen farm.

"Where are we headed?" Carolyn asked Odette, three days later, as Carolyn backed the Buick around to head down the long Quillen drive. It was early on a Thursday morning in August, and because Odette had been so insistent that she join her, Carolyn put off hockey practice until Friday.

"We're going to the river to my home territory, Oak Orchard. It's a BIG day there all day, and it won't be quite normal, but we'll have fun. Did you pack a swimsuit and a change of clothes?"

"Yes, mother", Carolyn quipped. "So tell me what this 'Big Thursday' celebration is all about."

"Well, it's a combination of things. First, it's an end of summer get together for Sussex Countians to enjoy the Indian River, sing and dance, and of course, eat and drink. The event began years ago and became an easy way for folks to pay their county taxes since the Assessor's Office always had a table. Big Thursday also marks the beginning of the oyster season, meaning local incomes get a boost. That's why the taxmen come to the happy event to get their due. You'll see them there today."

Carolyn had finally found the right opportunity to ask Odette about "her people." Odette shared that she was a Native American of the Nanticoke Tribe. She was raised in Oak Orchard, Delaware on the Indian River, which "her people" had dominion over until Europeans moved in. They had their own school and tribal grounds.

Oak Orchard was teeming with folks who had come in vehicles of every description, including wagons, bicycles, scooters, farm trucks, and cars. Carolyn parked the Buick in the grass under a large maple and hoped it would survive the bustle. At riverside, so much was happening that Carolyn blinked and focused left, then right, seeing 180 degrees of action everywhere. She scanned several large piers extending 100 to 500 feet into the river, covered with families sitting with their feet dangling in the water, or swimming, or racing between the pier boundaries. It was a hot August day, with the humidity just beginning to rise. Noises of excited youth echoed off the water and Carolyn's heart quickened, remembering her competitive swimming days.

They stopped by a vendor, ordered two cups of black coffee and split an order of eggs and scrapple. Since it was early, they found a space at one of the picnic tables near the river. "See that bathhouse over there?" Odette pointed out. "That's where you can change your clothes before and after swimming. It just costs a little, and is better than changing in the Buick. The next pier over has a great restaurant and by lunchtime there will be music. I'll come back by then and we can have lunch together."

"You mean you are leaving?" Carolyn said a bit surprised.

"Yes, after a while, as soon as you get the 'lay of the land.' I want to talk with my brother about a family matter and visit with my mother. Neither had to work at their regular jobs today since it's a Sussex County holiday, but I imagine they are busy with their own concessions at Clark's Beach. I'll find them soon."

When they parted ways, Carolyn changed into her swimsuit in the bath house and headed for the nearest pier. She slid into the cool water and breathed a relaxed sigh of contentment. Then she crawl stroked to the end of the pier several times and back. It was a good workout.

"Miss Brogan, is that you?" came a small voice seated dockside. Carolyn looked up to see the young girl who had been a "catcher" with the vaccinating crew. "You sure are a good swimmer."

"Hi, Ruthie*, is that you*?" Carolyn mimicked, happy that she could come up with a name.

"Yes, I'm Ruth Davis, a member of the other ninth grade homeroom, 9A. I thought it was you the other morning, but I was so busy catching that I didn't have time to say 'hi'. Sure didn't know you lived at the Quillen farm."

"Well, so nice to officially meet you, Ruth. Have you been in the water yet?"

"I just had a peanut butter and jelly sandwich for breakfast and my mother says I have to stay out of the water for a bit. Our whole family will be here until late this evening. Big Thursday is my favorite day of the year."

"This is my first time at Big Thursday, so I'm in awe of the goings on," Carolyn confessed.

"Be sure to ride the carousel before you leave. It's two piers upriver from here and shiny new! Just brought in from Baltimore, and it has the coolest music," Ruthie gushed.

"Thanks, I'll give it a go. See you later."

Carolyn swam around to a second swimming area between the next two piers. In the distance, she could see the shiny new carousel housed under a pavilion at the end of the next pier, which was very wide. Contented, she floated on her back and enjoyed the glorious warmth of the sun. Heat never seemed to burn her skin and she loved how quickly she tanned. Once out of the water, Carolyn sat in the sun watching the water traffic. Boats of all sizes were crisscrossing the river bringing more happy families to the festival. Sail boats, speed boats, row boats, fishing skiffs; there was even a police boat among the flotilla. Further downriver, she could see some canoe races in progress. After the sun dried her suit, she went back to her locker, left her towel, and put on a white shirt and blue Bermuda shorts over her suit. She planned to swim a lot more after lunch.

As she walked to lunch at George Buchanan's Restaurant, Carolyn noticed many families crabbing along the shoreline. Others had broken out picnic baskets and were enjoying fare brought from home. One family had just returned from a boat trip across the bay, and showed her the bushel of clams they raked up near Irons Lane. Carolyn could see there were many ways to have lunch in Oak Orchard.

Just as she was about to step up onto Buchanan's Pier, Carolyn did a double take as she spied a tall blonde male figure. It was the young West Virginia Reverend from Carey's Camp. On an impulse, she headed for the picnic table where he had just seated himself.

"Hello-o-o-oh-O!" Carolyn stammered as she realized the man who turned to face her was a different person. "Oh, I am so sorry. I thought you were someone else."

"Well, it's perfectly OK, the big blue eyes replied. Perhaps I'd prefer to be someone else," the eyes twinkled, looking head to toe at Carolyn. "Would you like to join us? "

"That's so kind of you, but I'm meeting someone out on the pier. Please, don't get up. Sorry to have interrupted your lunch," Carolyn replied as she sheepishly headed off towards Buchanan's Restaurant.

"That's the story of my life," the freckled face said, to the laughter of his two friends.

Carolyn and Odette ordered fried oysters and chicken salad and washed it all down with glasses of lemonade and iced tea, topped off by apple pie a la mode. They split the dessert, and Carolyn insisted on paying. It was a gorgeous afternoon and the river breeze was cool and refreshing for August. The usual heat and humidity had not materialized.

"I'm so glad you convinced me to come, Odette.

This place is rejuvenating. Sometimes you don't know that you need a break until you take one."

"I agree. Coming home to the river always gives me energy. Most days it is very peaceful and tranquil here, and I utterly relax as I listen to the waves lap against the piers. Of course, Oak Orchard has always been home to me, so I'm not objective."

"Did you find your mom and Leonard?" Carolyn inquired.

"Leonard was busy running canoe races for our youth, and mother was staffing our craft booth where we sell our handmade items to fund our Nanticoke Museum."

"Like baskets and moccasins? Do you know how to make all those things?"

"Sure, I've been making them since I was a kid," Odette laughed. But lately I've been replaced by younger hands now that I'm into chickens."

Just after Carolyn handled the check, a young man wearing a Coast Guard uniform strode over to their table. "Oh, that was fast! Odette exclaimed. Last I saw, you were in a bathing suit. Carolyn, I'd like you to meet my brother, Leonard Wright."

"What an honor to meet you. You have a wonderful person for a sister," Carolyn replied.

"Odette has told me some about you, but I wanted to meet you myself. Is my little sister behaving herself on most days?"

"She's the one keeping me straight, since you asked. And she did me a real favor bringing me to the river today." The three exchanged more pleasantries and then Leonard asked if he could have a few minutes alone with Odette. Odette and Carolyn agreed to meet at the Indian River Hotel pier in half an hour, and brother and sister walked off down the pier, arm in arm.

Carolyn wasn't far from the new carousel so she chose a white spotted pony and hopped on. As Ruthie had judged, the new merry-go-round had a lively sound that was a combination of calliope, organ, and percussion. The music put Carolyn in a carefree mood. Soon the up and down spinning motion created a soothing breeze against her face, while the rhythmic music and full tummy made her eyelids sag. Two times the carousel stopped to let people on and off, but Carolyn just sat still with her eyes closed, her head rested against the aluminum pole, enjoying it all.

Abruptly her tranquility was broken by a somewhat familiar voice saying, "Did your friends abandon you to the ups and downs of the carousel?" It was blue eyes, and he seemed taller now that he was fully standing.

Quick to recover, Carolyn parlayed, "What happened to all *your friends*?"

"They left me to fend for myself. My name is Jim Kelley and I'd sure like to know your name."

"Of course, guess I owe you one. I'm Carolyn Brogan, a new teacher at Selbyville School. I've been in Sussex County about a month. I call Philadelphia home."

"Well, you picked a good time to come south. What do you think of Big Thursday?" Jim inquired to keep the conversation going.

'It's a happening. Anything with water and food holds my attention," Carolyn smiled. They continued to chat and missed the next chance to leave the carousel. Jim said he was from Delmar, Delaware, about an hour southwest. He said he currently had a government job and worked in Lewes, a town which Carolyn had read about but never visited.

Eventually they disembarked from the merry-go-round and walked toward another pier where the sound of a nickelodeon was blaring from a pavilion. As they approached, Carolyn read the sign "Spear's Pavillion and Dance Hall." Inside, the floor was crowded with couples jiving to Glenn Miller's "Pennsylvania Six-Five Thousand'. Carolyn felt the pilings under the pavilion shake and the floor boards sway up and down with rhythm, as feet pounded the floor. She saw quite a few girls dancing with girls. Whenever the music stopped, someone would drop in a nickel, and another "hit" would boom out.

Jim took a step out on the floor and started a Lindy hop, motioning for her to join him. The dance was a quick one and Carolyn followed Jim's lead but found herself improvising as the music allowed. They did a half Charleston, part Lindy, part make-it-up-as-you-go routine that left them both laughing. It was the most fun Carolyn had had in a long time.

Huffing some, they grabbed a seat by the wall to recover. Carolyn found herself talking about how much she liked to swim and how much she missed competitive swimming and tennis matches. Jim was a good listener and was even better at asking her questions to move the conversation to a new topic. He had a great laugh that made his blue eyes sparkle.

"What brought you to Sussex County from Philadelphia?" he asked. Carolyn paused, not sure how to answer, when she spied Odette making a bee line for them across the dance floor.

'Oops," Carolyn warned. "Jim, here comes my friend and I've lost track of the time. Jim Kelley, meet my roommate, Odette Wright. Odette, this is Jim Kelley from Lewes."

"Glad to meet you, Jim. I thought Carolyn had drowned from all the fried oysters we ate at lunch. "

"So sorry I missed our appointed rendezvous, Odette. Guess this is my day to apologize to everyone. I can see by your face that we need to leave so you can be on time for your evening engagement. Right?"

"Yes, so right, regrettably," Odette sighed. "The day has been all too short."

"Indeed it has," Jim chimed in. Carolyn, I hope I can see you again so I can treat you to a basket of our Sussex County fried chicken. As a city girl, you might not know that we have lots of chickens in Sussex County."

"No, really? I'll take you up on that sometime."

CHAPTER SEVEN

In the least attractive places there is much art, if in the heart of the artist there is art. And here again the humility of self is desired such that the mind and senses are so overpowered by the wonders of a scene that the artist is compelled to paint.

- Jack Lewis

Jim and Rocco had been in Lewes a year and a half, and most of that time had been spent in the salt marshes battling mosquitos. Today they were down in a ditch training new C.C.C. recruits who invariably arrived every six months. Both men were shirtless, exposing their well-developed muscles. They wore suspenders to hold up loose work trousers that were partly rolled over brown, government-issue boots. The idea was to look powerful and ignore any blood or welts on their arms and backs. Being a Delaware native, Jim was almost immune to mosquito bites, and hardly noticed. But Rocco had to try hard to pretend that the mosquitoes weren't swarming around him, particularly since it was Rocco's turn to be "down" and use the "potato fork" to sling the sod. Today Jim was the "cutter." He stood above Rocco, facing him. First Jim raised his long, flat cutting spade and plunged it down into the matted marsh grasses. Then as Rocco hooked the wet clump that Jim had just loosened, Jim leaned back on his spade to raise the 60-80 pound chunk, and Rocco slung the chunk of sod upwards to one side of the ditch. From months of practice, they had perfected their technique, making drudgery look effortless. The new boys were always impressed.

Plunge, hook, lean, sling, the four motions occurred seamlessly in a one-two count. An experienced two man crew could complete 235 feet of ditch a day. Jim and Rocco were pros, and could cut more than that, but they no longer needed to since as Foreman and Senior Leader, they were "in charge". After the demonstration, the group was divided and a second ditch was begun 150 feet away. By afternoon, a sense of competition had emerged, which told Jim that he and Rocco had done their jobs.

While Jim was packing up the tools and directing his men into the half-ton for transport back to camp, he spied a person standing alone off in the distance. Since no one in his right mind wanted to stand in the middle of a mosquito infested Delaware marsh, Jim sighed and told the trucks to leave without him so he could see why the man was on State property. Jim was drenched in sweat, tired, hungry, and couldn't wait to shower off, but he dutifully trudged toward the intruder. Jim had long ago put his shirt back on and covered his freckles with his brimmed C.C.C. cap. As he approached, he saw that the man also wore a government-issue cap.

"Howdy, what brings you to this piece of paradise?" Jim asked.

The man was tall and thin and he held a sketchpad in one hand. A wooden box full of art supplies rested at his feet.

"Hi, I'm Jack Lewis attached to MC-54 out of Magnolia. Colonel Corkran has assigned me to paint scenes of men working at three of the Mosquito Control Sites in Delaware. On Monday, I'll be moving here for a three month stay before I head to MC-55 in Leipsic.

"You mean they pay you to sit and sketch while the rest of us bums dig ditches?" Jim said smiling.

"Afraid so. It may have something to do with the fact that Colonel Corkran's wife is a real patron of the arts." Jim remembered the W.P.A. Theater he had seen years earlier in Washington Square, New York City, and recalled that President Roosevelt, and especially *Mrs. Roosevelt,* had insisted artists, dancers, and actors be included in C.C.C. projects.

"Welcome to Lewes. I'm Jim Kelley, the Foreman for three of the MC-51 squads. We'll look forward to you joining us soon. "Did you walk all the way in here?"

"Sure did. Now that it's cooling off, I'll sketch until dinnertime, and then bum a ride back to Magnolia. I think I do my best work as the light fades out."

"Well, good luck. Nice to have met you. And, oh, you might want to slap on some bug balm if you have any. The mosquitoes get nasty at dusk."

As Jim walked the mile and a half back to camp, he humorously thought of how freezing it had been his first winter in Lewes. Even the ocean had frozen and the eerie sight of fog and crystalized foam blowing across the shoreline still haunted some of his dreams. That December, C.C.C. men built bulkheads and sand dunes, restored piers and boardwalks, and served as the first line of defense against nor'easters. Jim chuckled, wishing he could feel some of that biting cold right now. The cold would take away the mosquitoes and stifle the strong stench of the fish factories carried across town by the easterly breeze off the bay. The smell of Menhaden guts was always worse on a hot day like today.

As he strode toward the five C.C.C. barracks of Company 1224 that he and Rocco had helped lay out and build, he remembered his pride as each new camp building was constructed, a medical building, a canteen, officers' quarters, a kitchen, a supply room, and a bathhouse. As Foreman, Jim could recite the rules forwards and backwards for the 25 men of each barrack who were responsible for keeping the stove burning and for making sure their cots and foot lockers were spotless and "by the book." The "Army" protocol in Lewes was the same for Jim as it had been in Idaho, at Blackstone, and even in the Adirondacks. U.S. Government regulations were all he could ever remember living under. Seeing artist Jack Lewis and his sketchpad made Jim long for the museums and theaters he had loved in Philadelphia and New York City. It was like another life on a distant planet.

An important letter was waiting for Jim when he returned to his barracks, after the long-awaited shower. His inquiry to a California C.C.C. camp posting had been answered. The letter confirmed a six month assignment for Senior Leader Nicholas "Rocco" Zarrillo with C.C.C. 281, Camp SES-2, Fire Control, in Arroyo Grande, California. Concurrently Jim felt relief and sadness. Rocco now had job security, but Jim was losing his best friend. Two years, or four six month stints in the C.C.C. was the limit, and Rocco was at that point. He was still young enough to qualify, but the Delaware Mosquito Control Commission had its rules. California was forming a new soil conservation camp and greatly desired an experienced Senior Leader to train the new enrollees. Rocco was the best; California had no problem taking him. Jim's heart sank a bit.

Jim had dealt with the age regulations a year earlier by joining the Army Reserves. Because he was older than C.C.C. regulations allowed, Jim enlisted in the Reserve Corps of the U.S Army for three years. It solidified his selection as Foreman, which gave him more money. But mainly, it provided him more job security since Reserve Officers were often assigned to administer C.C.C. camps.   Now Jim really was in the Army, albeit the Reserve branch. He thought his drill instructor at Blackstone Military Academy would finally be proud of him.

There was a second letter waiting for Jim, one that concerned him greatly. It was sent to Capt. Helmer Swenholt, the Company Commander of 1224, Jim's boss, from Col. W.S. Corkran, the Head of the Delaware Mosquito Control Commission, the big boss. First Sergeant Jim Kelley and Acting Duty Sergeant Nick Zarillo had caused Col. Corkran public embarrassment because they had reported in the *Delaware Coast News* and the *Wilmington Evening Journal* that two administrators of Delaware mosquito control camps had "visited their respective homes last week." Since both men hailed from New Jersey, the article gave the impression that "our foremen are all Jerseymen and spend every spare minute and dollar they have in another state." Capt. Swenholt was being directed to submit all future items of news interest to a Mr. Messick of Col. Corkran's office who would make the release to the press, not Jim.

Tired as he was, Jim's blood pressure rose and his face turned red. He was "getting his Irish up" as his Mother used to say. As he thrust the letter of reprimand onto his bed and hurried to stand up and head off to find Rocco, a searing pain shot through Jim's lower back and down his left leg. Next thing he knew, he was laying on the floor beside his cot. Pain radiated across his back and the spasms made movement impossible. It had happened before, on days when he had been 'down in the ditch,' but never to this debilitating degree.

"Don't move, I'll go get some ice from the galley," came Rocco's life-saving command. Rocco grabbed the bed pillow and inserted it carefully under Jim's head. "I'll also get Smitty because he can keep his mouth shut, and bring him back to help me get you back in bed. Don't you dare try it yourself!" On the way out, Rocco made sure the accordion screen sectioning off the Foreman's area from the rest of the barracks was closed.

Jim was able to compose himself in the few minutes it took for Rocco and Smitty to return with the ice. The back spasms lessened a bit as he willed his legs to relax, but both letters were "downers." Life without Rocco would be duller and no doubt hurt his work quality. What a time for his back to go out and to receive a slap on the wrist from his superiors.

With delicate leverage, Rocco and Smitty hoisted Jim's 6'2" frame off the floor and into bed. Smitty departed and Rocco drew up a chair.

"I've got great news for you," Jim winced in his most cheerful voice. "You're accepted into the 281 at Arroyo Grande. Report date is in two weeks. Congratulations!" Talking, and even breathing, hurt Jim's back terribly, and he forced himself to smile through the pain. Rocco whooped with joy, and Jim could see the relief and adventure in his eyes as Rocco learned that his transfer to California was secure.

"Sure gonna miss you though," Jim whispered, as Rocco hurried away to share the news.

It took Jim's back the better part of two weeks to heal. The Camp Doctor ordered him to stay in bed with a pillow under his knees, which gave Jim valuable time for reading and thinking. Where was his life going?

He longed to return to college to finish his Bachelor's degree and get a "real job." However, jobs for a jeweler experienced in blister rust and mosquitoes were not likely to be posted anywhere. But then, neither were any other jobs, *anywhere,* likely to be posted. Would this terrible depression ever end?

"Mosquito Control, Lewes, 1936, by C.C.C. artist Jack Lewis, is oil on canvas, used with permission from the U. S. National Archives and Records Administration and the Delaware Division of Historical and Cultural Affairs.

Lewes Layout Squad for C.C.C. Delaware Mosquito Control Camp 1224. Jim Kelley is pictured fourth from right. Photo from Jim Kelley's scrapbook with permission from the National Archives and Records Administration and the Delaware State Archives.

Jim Kelley, center front, with C.C.C. shovel brigade, location unknown. From Jim Kelley's scrapbook. Rocco Zarrillo is believed to be the man with the dark cap, hands together, seated on Jim's right.

CHAPTER EIGHT

We are strong in the hard things that we do.

- Jack Lewis

Odette's evening engagement that summoned them from Big Thursday was tending the chicks, who now were covered with white feathers, had sprouted wings, and no longer twittered. The chickens demanded more mash as they grew, and, as soon as Carolyn's Buick arrived at the farm, Odette literally ran to refill the fountains that were so crucial in the August heat.

"I think we're going to need blocks of ice if the heat continues," Odette reported at dinner. "Although, I don't think it's just the heat that's causing us to lose a few each day." Carolyn could see the worried look on Cora's face. George was stoic, not wanting to verbalize any negatives, and as usual, just said, "pass the lemon butter, if you don't mind." They expected

Tuesday's mail to contain written analysis from the State Lab on the tissue samples and include some recommendations from the agricultural agent who had recently inspected all three chicken houses.

Cora was more than a little bit queasy about the lines of credit they had received from local hatcheries and feed companies. Half of their biddies had come from Indian River Breeding Farm and half from Elliott Evans and George Ellis whose canal side hatchery sold Barred Rock and New Hampshire chicks, instead of the "favorite" Rhode Island Reds. Odette kept written records on the difference in weight, vitality, and mash consumption of each variety, and made sure they remained in separate "rooms" of the chicken house. Then there was accumulating credit they owed to Tioga and Red Comb Feed Companies in Ocean View who supplied the mash, and a rolling balance to Jack Hill, owner of a local burlap bag business that recycled their used feed bags. Last week they had made partial payment to Steele and Keen who supplied the vaccinating crew as a preventative measure against the dreaded trachaeitus. The unpaid bills made Cora nervous, but she was thankful for the extension of trust that locals gave each other. Chickens and eggs had historically been women's work, and it was natural for Cora to assume the duty of keeping the running balance. Only she knew how much they owed on any given week. Most of the debts would not be settled until buyers, bidders, and weighmasters had done their jobs, and the Quillens were finally paid. The whole process could take about twelve weeks, if things went well.

In her nervousness, Cora was quizzing Odette again about the composition of the mash. Did she think the mixture was too heavy for the heat? Should they try a different supplier, even if it cost a little more? "I talked with my brother, Leonard today," Odette was telling Cora," and he says Lewes Fish Products Company is in the process of making a new and possibly more nutritious meal from menhaden fish caught off the Delaware Coast. The 'talk' on the water is that the demand for this new product will soon create lots more jobs."

"Will it cost more than what we use now?" Cora inquired.

"It's hard to say, but if I can use the phone, I'll call tomorrow and inquire about its availability and projected price."

"Of course, our phone is here for you whenever you need it, and Odette, see if they have tested this fish mash on live chickens yet."

Tuesday's mail brought the good news that tissue samples showed no signs of disease. Odette was also elated that the Quillen broiler practices had been rated "very good" to "excellent" on "cleanliness and sanitation." There was a brief celebration of joy and relief over second helpings of dessert at dinner. But concern prevailed, because chickens continued to die for no apparent reason.

A week later, Carolyn arose for school to find Odette's door closed. As she waited for her morning cup of tea to heat on their hot plate, she heard sobs coming from Odette's room. Given that it was already 7:15 and Odette was not downstairs filling fountains, something was terribly wrong.

'Odette, are you OK?" Carolyn said gently after a brief rap on Odette's door.

No answer. "Before I leave for the day, I just have to know that you are alright. Please, talk to me," Carolyn pleaded.

Slowly Odette's door opened.   Her eyes were swollen and her beautiful hair was tangled every which way. Surely she had been crying all night. Tears spilled down her cheeks, and she was unable to speak. Carolyn reached for Odette's hand and led her over to the bed and sat down. "I won't stay long. I just want to know what it is and how I can help."

"No one can help. They're all gone."

"Who?"

"The Lady and her husband,…. Cecile and Wilmer Steele……." Odette sputtered between gasps. Rather than ask if "gone" meant "dead," Carolyn sat quietly, waiting for Odette to continue.

"They're all gone….Last night they were on their boat with friends and it,…..it…..exploded. No one is alive," Odette shook some more with sobs.

'How awful.   I'm so sorry, Odette," Carolyn whispered, handing her a tissue. The two sat together while the tears flowed down Odette's cheeks. Seeing she was too weak to talk anymore, Carolyn brought her the cup of tea she had fixed for herself, hugged Odette, and closed the bedroom door again.

Carolyn made a beeline for Cora's kitchen. She

had been crying as well. "Guess you heard about the terrible accident," Cora mumbled. "I got a phone call at one o'clock this morning and woke Odette up to tell her. The poor girl has lost her second mother."

"No one survived?"

"Well, Wilmer and another man were rescued alive but so badly burned that…………It's just hard to believe. Since Wilmer is a State Senator, everyone knows them. And then there are the children."

"How many children did they have?"

"Four." Tears spilled over onto Cora's cheeks.

During homeroom, Principal Howie gave a prayer over the intercom for the Steele family. It was a long, sad day as hearts remained on the four absent students. Carolyn did not have any of the Steele's in her classes, but she did have some of their close friends who were in tears throughout the morning.

When she returned to the farm after hockey practice, Carolyn found Odette's room empty. She was not at the dinner table either, and Cora explained she had given Odette the night off to be with her brother. Leonard was best friends with Irwin Steele, the oldest son. Cora believed Leonard was now at the Steele's new family home in Ocean View, and there was a good chance Odette was there also. When Carolyn asked who would complete the evening feedings, Cora said she'd hired Billy Walker from the next farm over for one night and one morning's chores.

What a day. Carolyn felt drained, even though she knew none of the deceased. The apartment was all too quiet, so Carolyn did what she usually did to lift her spirits. She sat at the kitchen table and addressed an envelope to "Pottstown High School."

Dear Virginia,
So much has happened since my last letter, I hardly know where to begin. My roommate, Odette Wright is teaching me a lot about Sussex County, and about chickens. Who thought I'd ever be studying chickens? I can tell the difference between a Long Island Red and a Barred Rock. I'm learning about the different kinds of mashes (feed), and I've watched a vaccinating crew...

Carolyn opened her eyes and realized she had dozed off. She wanted to tell Virginia about Big Thursday and about the accident, but it would have to wait. She staggered toward her bedroom, remembering that tomorrow she had to administer the first Unit Test in English classes and then coach her hockey team at an away game in Millsboro.

During the next week, Odette dragged through her work chores and missed half her classes at Delaware State College. No matter how Carolyn and Cora tried to lift Odette's spirits, nothing seemed to help. Odette didn't want to talk to anyone, and she spent much time in her bedroom with the door closed.

"Honey, we're just going to have to give her some space, and pray to the good Lord that Odette can find her faith," Cora counseled Carolyn, who was beside herself with concern. But Cora was the one who had just said that she wasn't taking Odette's dinner to her room any longer. "I feel like I'm encouraging her to withdraw, and so I told her yesterday that if she wanted dinner tonight she'd have to come to the house," Cora confessed. "After all, it's been nearly two weeks."

Dinner that night was strained, but Odette's mental outlook brightened day by day, as was hoped. But Carolyn could see that Odette was still struggling inside. A few days later, Carolyn was awakened before daybreak to the sound of Odette coughing furiously. When the whooping sound didn't cease, Carolyn put on her bathrobe and found Odette hunched over the kitchen sink.

"I feel like I'm going to cough out everything I have inside," Odette said between gasps. What is wrong with me?" Acting like the mother, Carolyn pressed her hand against Odette's forehead.

"Wow, Odette, you've got a raging fever!" Carolyn exclaimed. "When did you start to feel bad?"

"I just woke up this way about a half hour ago."

"Well, here are two aspirin, and I'm going to get you the cough syrup I have in our bathroom," was Carolyn's directive. "Since today's Friday, I can be home in time to help you with the evening chores. Make sure you drink plenty of fluids today and rest whenever you can."

"Yes I will," was the weak response.

After school, Carolyn found Odette lying on the bathroom floor and retching every few minutes. "How can I throw up when I've hardly had anything to eat?" Odette moaned. "And I've got diarrhea too, how do you figure that?"

"Do you still have the fever?" Carolyn questioned.

"Maybe not so much, but I sure have a terrific headache," Odette managed to get out before collapsing onto the floor again.

"Odette, I'm going to ask Cora to take a look at you."

"She's gone."

"Gone where?"

"Her brother-in-law called at lunchtime and said Henrietta, Cora's sister, was in labor with their first child. Cora and George left in a rush to get to Georgetown before the baby comes."

"Darn, I was hoping she could make you some soup, or some tea with honey, or some secret Sussex County concoction to settle your stomach."

"Don't even mention food!" Odette pleaded.

"Look, Odette, I'm doing downstairs to start refilling the fountains and put out more mash. Then I'll return to check on you and get further instructions. You just get back in bed as soon as you can and get some sleep. Keep taking the aspirin, OK?"

"OK.....Carolyn, thanks."

The air hung heavy in the chicken house when Carolyn reached the bottom step. It was mid-September, but it felt like the 'dog days of summer.' No air was stirring, and the chickens were unusually quiet. Carolyn wondered if she should attempt to stir things up with Odette's chicken house shuffle, but instead she used a tin skuttle to pour water into the first fountain. There, only 150 more to go. The fountains were ceramic jars that sat on the sawdust floor, causing Carolyn to bend over, remove the fountain lid, fill the jar, and replace the lid before straightening up. Trips back and forth to the water tank to refill the skuttle were welcome relief for Carolyn's back muscles. By the time she reached the end of the second chicken house, her back muscles were screaming.

Carolyn looked at her watch which was covered with grit and sawdust. As she wiped it off, she was surprised to see it had taken her nearly two hours to fill the empty fountains. Most of the feed troughs were empty, and she needed to get them replenished. That shouldn't take as long, but Carolyn was uncertain which mash the Rhode Island Reds, Barred Rocks, and New Hampshire's received. She knew there was a different regimen for each. Light was fading and the chicken bays were poorly lit, because after sundown, chickens prefer the dark.

Carolyn went to the water tank, splashed water on her face, and then took a drink. That probably broke with the State sanitation code, but she was so thirsty, she couldn't help herself. Then she flew up the steps to ask Odette about the feed choices. Odette's bed was empty and Carolyn spied Odette still lying on the bathroom floor.

"Odette, girl, you've got to get back to bed." Carolyn's voice raised in alarm.

No answer.

"Odette, Odette, please open your eyes!" Carolyn nearly screamed. No answer. Carolyn felt for a pulse, and finally located a weak beat. "Oh my God, Odette, hold on until I can get an ambulance here. Hold on, I'll be right back," Carolyn implored as she rose to dash down the steps to the phone in the main house. Thank heavens, no one in Sussex County ever locked their doors.

It seemed like forever until the ambulance came. Carolyn sat beside Odette, wiping off her forehead with a damp cloth, whispering to her, and praying. The two ambulance attendants used all their strength to carry Odette's limp body down the steep steps of the chicken house apartment. Carolyn wanted to hop in the ambulance to be with Odette, but what could she really do at Beebe Hospital in Lewes? There was plenty for her to do at the farm.

Unbelieving, Carolyn watched the ambulance lights disappear down the long Quillen driveway. Now it was completely dark and the mash troughs were still empty. Carolyn surveyed the stacks of feedbags stored behind the bottom step, her favorite vantage point. Oh, to see clearly now. The markings on the burlap casings didn't mean much to Carolyn, so she strained to lift and open one 50 pound bag that she randomly selected. Surely she couldn't kill 12,000 chickens from one incorrect feeding.

CHAPTER NINE

Perspective is a natural way of composition. Nature has a way of composing. The artist can only select and might do well to follow nature like the canal in her effortless composing.

- Jack Lewis

Life without Rocco just wasn't the same. Under doctor's orders, Jim significantly altered his daily routine. Because he couldn't dig ditches, he spent more time in the social hall, gingerly testing his back on pool and ping-pong. Bonding with the new corpsmen was "required" and Jim often enjoyed it. Now he had extra time to scout out the new enrollees and try to develop a short list of replacements for Rocco's Senior Leader slot. Since Col. Corkran's letter of reprimand, Capt. Swenholt, had been cordial but cool toward Jim. Jim wanted to be sure that his recommendations to

Capt. Swenholt for Rocco's position were all sound choices. He couldn't afford any more mistakes.

Rocco left camp five days prior to his California report date so he could visit his family and Elaine in Jersey City. Elaine had a job as a secretary and couldn't afford to give it up to follow Rocco west. Not seeing each other every two weeks would be hard on the lovers, but they promised to write often and to telephone each other every Sunday.

Artist-in-residence Jack Lewis arrived and quickly gained a following of corpsmen eager to listen to his storytelling and to sing along at Jack's harmonica and accordion sessions after dinner. Jim could see that Jack was a natural leader, but his name would definitely stay off the short list since Jack's specialized assignment came directly from Col Corkran's wife.

One afternoon before Jim was cleared for regular duty, he accepted Jack's invitation to accompany him into the field. Jack liked to talk, and Jim never found talking to be a chore. As they chatted and walked toward town, Jim strengthened his stride to keep up with Jack's long legs. Jack had turned down an offer of a ride to the Lewes fishing wharf, saying walking gave him 'the lay of the land.' "Painting is all about perspective, just like life", Jack philosophized. "I paint most freely when I have some time to absorb my surroundings. Walking gives the best perspective." Jim was just happy to be back on his feet again, and he gratefully inhaled a deep breath of the cool September morning air, as the two men paced each other.

"So how did you get to be a Foreman?" Jack asked

Jim.

"After I dropped out of college and spent 2 years as a jeweler's apprentice in New York City, I did six months in Idaho in the St. Joe's Forest killing blister rust, then a winter at Camp Henlopen in beach replenishment, and now two terms digging mosquito trenches here at MC-51.   Along the way, I joined the Army Reserves, and kissed up to all the brass," answered Jim, his eyes twinkling.

"Well, the men respect you, so you must be doing something right."

"Thanks, so what about you, Jack?   What route brought you to Delaware in these uncertain times?"

"Oh, I fell asleep one day and woke up only when a beautiful maiden kissed me and told me to bring my brushes to Delaware."

"Does the beautiful maiden have a sister who could kiss me?" Jim retorted, respecting Jack's privacy. Perhaps in due time, Jack would feel comfortable talking about himself, or perhaps not. Maybe Jack just couldn't resist remaining an elusive spirit, like most of the actors and writers Jim had encountered in Philadelphia and New York.

Jack ignored Jim's quip and instead said how much he was looking forward to seeing the fishing boats today on the Lewes-Rehoboth Canal. "I've always loved boats," Jack shared, "and I think I can work some into the background of today's sketches. Our boys will be clearing out the drainage culvert that runs along the canal, and hopefully there will be boats nearby."

Sure enough, Jack set up his table on the road above the culvert with a panorama of boats docked behind the working corpsmen. Jim opened the wooden box containing Jack's pens, paints and brushes, and moved a distance away so Jack could find a starting point. The canal banks were crawling with Mosquito Control men raking, digging, and pulling out debris. They looked happy to be in town instead of in the marshes. Jim swatted a mosquito on his cheek and knew that if he had noticed, he must be far too idle. As Jim heard the work Foreman shout the orders, Jim felt unease, knowing that there were hundreds of young men eager for his job.

"Come take a look," Jack invited Jim after about twenty minutes.

"That's amazing. You work fast and it's already half finished. What are those grid lines for?" Jim inquired.

"You know how you section off your marshes and run the ditches 150 feet apart? Well, I use a grid of lines, sometimes dots, for the same reason---to keep things in proportion. The grid lines won't show in the finished painting, if there ever is such a thing."

Jim remembered the grids he had used on the Idaho hillsides fighting blister rust. "You mean this won't become the final painting?"

"Probably not. I like to return with three or four good beginnings, and then finish in my studio. Say, I could really use a better lit space than the storage closet I've just been assigned. Do you think that would be possible?"

"Now I know the real reason why you wanted me

to carry your supply box," Jim said, his pearly whites gleaming. "I'll see what I can do."

Jim soon realized that Jack preferred people beside him as he painted. Having an audience appeared to inspire Jack, not distract him. Perhaps Jack was not the elusive soul Jim had him pegged for. He certainly was no introvert.

On the return walk to camp, their conversation quickened. "I owe my job to Eleanor Roosevelt; God bless her," Jack said. "If she hadn't insisted, painters, actors, and playwrights would have been omitted from the legislation. For me to graduate and not find work would have been so discouraging. I owe her so much."

"You have a college degree?" Jim asked a little wistfully.

"Yep, from Rutgers".

Jim's silence and melancholy demeanor was not unnoticed by Jack, who Jim would soon learn missed nothing when it came to people or landscape. "What do you think about the C.C.C. now that you've succeeded up the ranks?" Jack parlayed, focusing on something positive.

"Like you, I'm so grateful for a job. It's not only the money, it's the sense of contributing something for the greater good. Know what I mean?"

"Sure do."

"But…," Jim went on, "it's a far cry from the military glories I imagined at Blackstone Military Academy. I'm afraid fighting mosquitoes has dampened my drive for a military career; but like I say, I'm thankful for all the work, and the pay."

"Well, we learn from every experience. My motto is 'keep messing around'. I say that 'I paint for the trash can,' and I don't fear mistakes because my errors make me a much better artist."

Jim was impressed with Jack's resolute, but cheery, outlook on life. He didn't realize it yet, but Jim had just heard the first of Jack Lewis' many philosophies. It seemed the artist was more than a painter. But it did occur to Jim that Jack Lewis had the knack for making him feel happy, somewhat like Rocco Zarrillo.

CHAPTER TEN

Work — especially constructive or creative work — is a never-failing friend.

- Jack Lewis

Carolyn tossed in bed, worried about Odette. Finally she gave up the pretense of sleep, and got up to fix a stiff cup of coffee. Thank goodness it was Saturday and she didn't have school to contend with. To clear her head, Carolyn, ever the organizer, made a list:

1) call Billie Walker and hire him for Saturday and Sunday

2) complete the morning chores

3) call the hospital to check on Odette

4) look for a phone number for Cora's sisters and tell George and Cora about Odette

5) make sure to eat a meal

When it was barely light enough to see, Carolyn

began to check the fountains and the feed troughs. She refilled the first "room" of the bay, and then stopped to use the kitchen phone so she could hire Billy Walker. When Billy's Mother answered, she told Carolyn that Billy was headed to Newark to enjoy the University of Delaware's opening football game against West Chester. Carolyn steadied her voice, and thanked her. She also had the presence of mind to ask Mrs. Walker if she could give her the phone number of Ruthie Davis.

Within the hour, Ruthie arrived on her bike. Carolyn hugged her, and told Ruth she was so grateful that she could come at a moment's notice. Carolyn said she'd pay her more since it was a weekend. To herself, Carolyn quaked inside because she knew she was entrusting the welfare of the whole operation to a ninth grader. Ruthie was small for her age, but she was a real worker. She filled the fountains quickly and calmed Carolyn's unease with local chatter. Ruth didn't know much about the different kinds of mash, but she agreed with Carolyn that any short term "miss-feed" probably wouldn't matter.

By nine o'clock, Carolyn was drenched in sweat. The day was going to be another September scorcher, and Carolyn was alarmed by the six chicken carcasses she collected on the morning rounds. Ruthie was still out back covering over the burial mound the two had dug at the property line. Carolyn decided to keep one carcass, just in case Odette wanted to send it to Georgetown or Dover for lab work.

The sound of a truck in the driveway sent Carolyn outside.

"Good morning, Miss Brogan," the man said, striding toward her to shake her hand, ignoring her grimy fingers. "I'm Jack Hill from Hill and Korngold's." Carolyn smiled and remembered she had met him recently at a school Parents Night since his daughter, Gladys, was enrolled in Carolyn's ninth grade English class. Realizing that Carolyn didn't know why he'd come, Mr. Hill clarified, "I've come to pick up the bags."

"The bags?"

Yes, I come every two weeks to collect your used feed bags. We have a shaker machine in our store, and then we bundle them in units of 50 and send them to Philadelphia for reconditioning. You get a credit for returning them to us."

"Oh, I see," Carolyn said as she turned to collect the bags by the steps she had emptied since yesterday afternoon.

"Where's Odette?" Jack Hill asked.

"An ambulance took her to Beebe last night. She was in a real bad way. I'm hoping to know something about her status before too long."

"Sorry to hear about that. I heard she was devastated by the Steele tragedy." Jack Hill paused, and then said, "I know where she stacks her empty burlaps," as he headed off toward the barn.

"Oh, thank heavens."

Carolyn saw Mr. Hill off and then went to Cora's kitchen to call the ice company. It was Saturday, and she hoped she could arrange a delivery before the end of the day. How many blocks should she order? Perhaps the ice company had records from earlier deliveries? First, Carolyn rooted around in the kitchen drawer where the phone book was lodged, hoping to find a number for Cora's sister. No luck, but then why would Cora have to write down her only sister's phone number.

As the ice truck arrived in the heat of the day, Carolyn gave a sigh of relief at the sight of the men off- loading the large blocks into the shade of the new chicken house. Carolyn signed the delivery slip, knowing this would be another expense to increase Cora's anxiety. Now she and little Ruthie would have to figure out how to move twelve 80 pound blocks of ice to the proper spots. But first, they each plopped down and sat on an ice cube for as long as they could, while giggling their heads off.

"Oh my, it sure feels good-oh-oho-c-c-cold!" they squealed at each other.

"I don't even mind my pants being wet, it feels delightful," Carolyn said, hopping up to survey the chicken house for anything to help move the slippery cubes.

"Ruthie, go see if you can find anything with wheels in the other houses."

Carolyn had no luck searching for an ice hook or other tool to lift the blocks. Ruthie found a kid's wagon in the barn and offered it as a partial solution. After a second canvas of the barn, Carolyn discovered a leather harness that she could position around her shoulders and under the block. By bending her knees and pulling upward she could lift the ice enough for Ruthie to slide the wagon underneath. Then, with the help of gravity, the block could be rolled into the wagon, which amazingly held the weight. With both of them pulling and pushing, Carolyn and Ruthie set the block in the first "room" of Rhode Island Reds. Immediately the chickens gathered around it. So that was how it worked. Now to do that eleven more times.

At two o'clock, Carolyn apologized to Ruthie and took her to Cora's kitchen so they could make lunch. They still had three ice blocks to position, but Carolyn was famished as she realized that she had only accomplished one item off her early morning list. Bless Cora, Carolyn found some of Cora's famous chicken salad in the ice box, and soon the two were eating chicken salad and lettuce on rye with lemonade and chocolate chip cookies. Just as they were finishing lunch, the phone rang. Carolyn jumped from the unexpected loud sound, and realized she had been a country girl too long. It was Cora's high pitched voice on the other end, talking so fast that Carolyn could hardly make out the words.

"We are at Beebe, and we've just seen Odette. She's still unstable, but she was conscious enough to know we are here. My sister had difficulty with her labor, and her Georgetown doctor sent her to Beebe Hospital last night. We followed her ambulance here. She's still in the delivery room, and they won't let me in," Cora paused to get her breath. Before Cora rushed back to the maternity ward, she told Carolyn they planned to stay until the baby came. Cora said it was a blessing that she and George could be with Henrietta and Odette at the same time, and then Cora quickly asked how things were at the farm. Carolyn assured her all was well, and told Cora that she had Odette's duties down pat.

As Carolyn and Ruthie opened the kitchen door to return to work, Carolyn was greeted in the driveway by another man who had just stepped out of his truck.

"Hi, I'm Homer Pepper from H & H Poultry in Selbyville, and I've come to look over your brood."

"You... you're a buyer?" Carolyn stammered.

"Yes, that would be me. H & H would like the chance to bid on your poultry lot. I'll just have a look around, if you don't mind."

Well, Carolyn did mind, because she didn't know the first thing about how the bidding and buying process worked, but she was sure it was the most crucial step of all. And Carolyn felt uneasy about how Mr. Pepper's eyes peered at her. From nightly dinner discussions, she recalled the names of two Ocean View poultry companies, Bill Vickers, and Powell & Turner, but H & H was new to her.

"Of course, feel free to look at our chickens. Ruthie, show him the new house first, and then the others, Carolyn said, shooting Ruthie a 'keep an eye on him' look. "George and Cora are out of town today, but I'm sure they will consider any offer your company would make."

Carolyn paced back and forth in her apartment until she heard Homer Pepper's truck leave the farm. She intended to stay away from the man, lest he think she was the person raising the chickens. The way he eyed her, Carolyn was sure he knew she was from out of town.

"What did he say, anything?" Carolyn questioned Ruthie.

"Not much. He picked up chickens in each house and examined them. He looked over the bags of mash and said he wanted to know what our feeding regimen was. Said he'd call Cora soon to get his questions answered. And, oh, he eyed the blocks of ice."

"Did he see the dead chicken I'd set aside for the lab?" Carolyn asked.

"Yes, I think he did. But he didn't ask me about it. Like I say, his eyes took everything in, but his mouth stayed closed."

"Thanks, Ruthie. You are a very mature young lady for a ninth grader. Now let's finish moving those last three blocks of ice."

After completing the evening chores, Carolyn slept like a log. Sunday morning dawned hotter than ever. Carolyn put on the oldest clothes she had, and went downstairs to start the routine of fountains and feed. Ruthie would not be joining her until afternoon since she was committed to play the organ in church.

Most of the ice blocks had melted away, and Carolyn noticed the chickens appeared energized and more hungry than normal. Too bad Homer Pepper wasn't around, but she was sure he wasn't working on a Sunday. By mid-afternoon when Ruthie arrived, Carolyn was starting to fatigue. Her back ached from Saturday's ice block moving and she was covered in saw dust, corn meal, and grime. Her hair was wet from sweat and she smelled strongly of ammonia.

"Ruthie, let's start the evening feedings early so I can have a couple hours to prepare for my English classes tomorrow. Why don't you start on the fountains, and I'll do the mash. OK?"

"OK." Ruthie was all energy in spite of the two miles she had just peddled.

Carolyn was bending over a feed trough, skuttle in hand, when a man's voice startled her to a quick stand.

"Well, I guess you might know a thing or two about chickens after all," said the tall blonde man dressed in his Sunday go to church clothes. He looked quite handsome. A few seconds elapsed before Carolyn recognized Jim Kelley from Oak Orchard. He had a sheepish smile on his face and was waiting for her to say something.

"In my condition, I sure can't deny it," Carolyn said, trying not to look totally alarmed that he had found her in such a state of slime. "Of course, this is my second job, and I only do it for people I really like. Remember, Odette who I introduced you to at the river? She's in the hospital, and I'm tending her chickens."

"Sorry to have startled you. I spent the day with my parents in Delmar, and took my Mother to church since it's her birthday today. After calling your school to get your address, I realized I could return to Lewes this route and drop by. I should have called first," Jim apologized. "When I drove up the driveway, I could see that this was a poultry farm, and knew how wrong I'd been…..about the chicken remark," Jim added, still smiling a wide grin that exposed the biggest white teeth Carolyn had ever seen.

"Yes, Odette and I had a real good laugh on the drive home over your comment, so don't apologize. I'm happy you stopped by because, except for my little helper Ruthie, I've been alone all weekend. It's nice to have another adult to talk with," Carolyn said nonchalantly, hoping Jim wouldn't notice how uncomfortable she felt looking so ghastly.

"I'll be back in a minute," Jim said. "Need to get something from my vehicle." Jim returned, without his suit jacket, holding a set of work fatigues. "I never leave home without a change of clothes. Excuse me again," Jim said as he walked out of sight into the next "room" of the bay before Carolyn could ask what he was doing.

Although hidden from view, Jim kept talking. "I really came to ask you to go back to Oak Orchard with me next Saturday evening to listen to some jazz. The river is totally different at night, and I think it would be a fun evening. What do you say?"

When he reappeared wearing the fatigues, Jim already had a skuttle in hand. He set the pail down, easily lifted the 50 pound feedbag at Carolyn's feet, and filled the skuttle with the No. 5 mash. "Now, Miss Brogan, please direct me to the next trough. You look a little tired and worn out, and I am a 'local experienced man' who is eager to help."

"You are very kind with your adjectives, Mr. Kelley. I am, after all, an English teacher," Carolyn countered.

Laughing and talking, they filled all the troughs before Ruthie finished the fountains. While they lugged water to the remaining jars, Jim reminded Carolyn she hadn't given him an answer about Saturday night. "I accept with pleasure," Carolyn said, "and I promise to take a shower before we meet again."

Later that night, Carolyn had time to reflect on the day and was impressed that Jim Kelley had taken the time to search her out and stop by. And she was even more surprised that he wanted to see her again, given their sweltering Sunday afternoon encounter.

CHAPTER ELEVEN

At the moment when, after long, fruitless laboring, precisely the right subject enters the scene and takes precisely the right posture at precisely the right spot, one enters the exalted plane of a painting experience and realizes the fact of everything being so precisely right is a fact of spiritual health and inspiration.

- Jack Lewis

Carolyn was waiting for Jim on the front porch of the farmhouse when he arrived for their jazz night at Indian River. "Wow, you clean up well," Jim blurted out as he opened the screen door. Carolyn's dark shiny hair fell onto one shoulder and was pinned back on the other side of her face. Her tan skin gleamed against her white halter neck sundress.

"Should I bring anything else?" Carolyn asked,

holding her navy cardigan sweater.

"No, I think I have all we need in the truck," Jim said, and thought to himself, "you are quite enough." On the drive north to Millsboro, Jim asked how Odette was feeling, and then how the chickens were doing. Odette was home from the hospital and her system had fought off the virus, but she was still 'down' about the death of Cecile Steele. The chickens were doing better now that the weather had cooled a bit. True to form, Jim controlled the conversation by asking the questions, and enjoying Carolyn's every word. With ease, he navigated the flow of topics, which were not about him.

"What have your students taught you so far?" Jim asked, his white teeth flashing as he smiled broadly.

"Yes, you're right, I'm learning far more from them at this early stage than they from me. Besides school, so many of my students have substantial farm duties and chores. Many of my ninth graders are already struggling with the decision about college. Besides the tuition cost, there's the loss of farm labor the family will suffer when the student leaves home."

Jim asked about her hockey team, and just as Carolyn began to get a bit nervous from all of Jim's questions, they arrived at Oak Orchard.

"The jazz won't start until well after sunset, so we have some time. Let's walk around and stretch our legs before we get on the water," Jim suggested.

"We're going on a boat ride?" Carolyn queried, her voice rising a bit.

"Yes, a dinner cruise. Quite upscale, but you'll see

soon enough," Jim smiled, gently touching her elbow as they stepped up onto the first pier. It was a quiet 'Indian Summer' evening, with a warm breeze barely causing ripples on the river. Carolyn could hear the Nickelodeon echoing down the beach from Spear's Dance Hall. She could hear voices from the tables at Buchanan's Restaurant, and smell the salt air seeping landward from the bay. Soon Carolyn began to relax, just like Odette said always happens in Oak Orchard.

"How about we do it once more with feeling?" Jim asked Carolyn.

"Pardon me?"

"What'd you say that we hop on the Carousel and continue where we left off last time," Jim proposed. "I like going in circles, since I've been doing it my whole life," Jim said, and then looked like he wished he hadn't.

"Sure, that would be fun," Carolyn said, hopping on a polka dotted unicorn, while Jim chose a palomino beside her. "Tell me about some of the circles you've traveled in," Carolyn requested.

"Oh, I fell asleep one day and woke up only when a beautiful maiden kissed me and told me to join the Army Reserves in Delaware."   Carolyn expected him to continue, but instead, Jim just closed his eyes and started to hum with the music. After several more revolutions of the merry-go-round, Jim finally spoke. "I've done my time in Idaho in Roosevelt's Tree Army, and spent days in Delaware on sand dunes, salt marshes, and forests. It's been a long vacation in the outdoors, and I'll tell you more about my circles on our river ride," Jim said, as he grabbed her hand to jump off the carousel as it slowed.

When they returned to the truck, Carolyn was amazed by the items Jim had brought for their outing. In short order, he unloaded two pillows and a blanket, a basket with their dinner, two life vests, and a small ice chest. He handed her a bottle of bug splash and a small flashlight, "just in case we don't want to rough it," he explained.

"Are we spending the night?" Carolyn quipped.

"I wish," Jim moaned, "but reveille comes early."

"This way, Madame," Jim directed, as he lifted the ice chest with the dinner basket on top, after threading his arm through the two life vests. They walked a short way down the shore line to find a row boat waiting for them.

"Our cabin cruiser," Jim smiled. "One pillow is for your back rest, the second to sit on. I won't need them because I'm the motor. I suggest we take our shoes off now and stow them in the hull with the flashlight. Heavy objects go to the middle," Jim expounded as he set the ice chest and basket in the center of the boat."

"You give orders clearly," Carolyn noted.

"Lots of practice. Sorry if I sound like the drill Sergeant I've been. One of my circles."

After rolling up his pant legs, Jim helped Carolyn settle herself in the stern of the rowboat with one pillow as a backrest. Jim inserted the oars in the locks and walked the rowboat several feet away from shore. Then he deftly lowered his rear onto the center seat, facing Carolyn, and swung his long legs into the boat.

His added weight grounded the boat, but Jim pushed off shore again using one oar. Several seconds later, Carolyn felt the boat lunge forward as Jim took his first powerful stroke. Then Jim oared a second one that sent them smoothly gliding across Indian River just in time to watch the sunset.

The huge orange ball in the sky turned fiery red before disappearing, and its afterglow turned the sky all shades of aqua, pink, and crimson. The seagulls squawked the ending of light, and Carolyn could hear crickets and the chorus of night creatures harmonizing. The pull-glide, pull-glide, of Jim's smooth strokes, and the serenity of the twilight created a magical aura. Carolyn realized it was one of those perfect spaces of silence when words are useless. Silently, she gazed at Jim's moving shoulders and was thankful he had brought her here. She felt completely relaxed.

"That dock we just passed is "Clark's Beach," or "Riverdale," Jim finally broke the silence. "Your friend Odette and her brother Leonard use that beach. It's deeded to the Nanticoke Tribe."

"Strange that they should require a deed, given that they originally owned it all," Carolyn said, understanding that this was where Odette had gone to be with her mother. "Doesn't it bother you that we never see the Nanticokes, or, come to think of it, any of the colored people in Sussex County? In suburban Philadelphia, it's quite different."

"You chummed with the Indians in Philly?" Jim dragged his voice in feigned disbelief. "I lived in Philadelphia for two years, and I never saw any

Indians."

"Oh, you know what I mean. You lived in Philadelphia for two years?"

"Yes, a certified jeweler is rowing your boat. I'm a Peirce graduate. Another one of my circles."

Carolyn had never heard of Peirce, and she was still pondering the injustice of "sectioning off" the Delaware natives to one small portion of the riverbank, when she heard Jim's voice,

"A penny for your thoughts."

Well, that was more open-ended than Jim's usual questions. And it made responding a lot tougher. "Oh, I was just thinking about my best friend Virginia and the wonderful trip we took to Venice after our junior year in college. We had an Italian adventure to remember, and celebrated being momentarily free of school and our parents oversight. Virginia and I have been together since grade school, and I miss her."

"I just lost my best buddy to re-assignment on the west coast. It was my duty to sign the papers to send him to California, and it nearly killed me. We shared so much," Jim said wistfully, as Carolyn took note of the sadness in his voice.

Jim continued his pull-glide, pull-glide rhythm, which seem to mesmerize both of them. Carolyn closed her eyes and dipped a finger into the water, letting it make a silent wake as Jim oared. She breathed out a sign of contentment and hoped that the moment would never end.

"It won't be long now until we get close enough to drop anchor and have dinner. I'm beginning to get hungry," Jim almost whispered, so as not to disturb the tranquility. The moon had risen and in its subtle light Jim could sense that Carolyn's eyes were closed. He took the opportunity to stare at her beauty. His eyes lingered over her smooth shoulders and the white of her halter dress seemed to shimmer in the moonlight. From that moment on, he knew that he would never be the same. Whether or not he ever saw Carolyn Brogan again, he was in love.

Carolyn noticed that they were approaching some other boats. Jim turned on the flashlight and tied it to the bow stay. "A safety precaution," he said. "Perhaps I should have had you put on your life vest earlier," Jim said. "Do you swim?"

Carolyn giggled, remembering all the competitive swim races she had won in college, and replied, "Yes, I'm a good swimmer."

Jim threw their anchor overboard and opened the ice chest. On top of the ice, were two wine goblets, a bottle of white wine, and a container of water. Jim produced a corkscrew from the dinner basket, and popped open the bottle. Carolyn lifted the chilled goblets and held them steady as Jim poured. "To our health and strength in uncertain times," Jim toasted. Their glasses clinked together and they gingerly repositioned as the boat rocked on the gentle waves.

Quite a few more boats had joined them, some with lights that helped make dining less mysterious in Jim and Carolyn's boat. "Here, I promised you some Delmarvalous fried chicken awhile back, and I always make good on my promises," Jim said handing her a fried chicken leg and a napkin. "Just let me know when you want the next course. We have more chicken, potato salad, brownies, and a thermos of coffee."

"Foreman Kelley,... I am very impressed….. with the menu… and your organization," Carolyn earnestly mumbled between munches. "If the rest is as good as this chicken, I may join the Army Reserves."

"Well, I *am* a man of some authority, at least when it comes to mosquitos."

"What?"

"Oh, I'll explain later. It's another one of my circles."

The music started before they finished devouring their moveable feast. First it was just the saxophones and horns tuning up with short scales and 'toots.' Then the instruments synchronized and the soft sound of jazz floated across the water. The wind shifted toward them, and Carolyn realized that there was a large crowd of people assembled on the dockside pavilion and surrounding lawn. She could hear their many voices over the music.

"Where are we?" Carolyn asked.

"We're anchored off Rosedale Beach---Cotton Club South, or New Orleans North, ---whatever you term it," Jim described. It's a huge new Hotel and Resort Complex. All the big names in jazz come here: Duke Ellington, Fats Waller, Louis Armstrong, Count Basie, Chick Webb, Ella Fitzgerald, and names I don't even know. It's high black jazz, and it's another world."

"You mean the resort is only for colored people?"

"Yes indeed. Now you know why they wouldn't want to waste their time in Oak Orchard," Jim said, stroking the oars again. "I think I'll be ok moving us toward shore a little more. They know we're out here anyway, and I'm certain more boats will be arriving, this being Saturday night."

As Jim propelled the boat closer, Carolyn was amazed at the hundreds of well-dressed dark skinned people assembled on the pier and on the front lawn of the hotel. She could see lots more people still dining inside. The musicians were playing under a brightly lit pavilion at the beginning of the boating and swimming area. A deep female voice bellowed out a sorrowful song that Carolyn didn't recognize, but she liked its haunting melody.

"Have you done this before?" Carolyn asked, and then laughed, "not that it's any of my business."

"I came one other evening with Rocco, my friend who just transferred to California. As good as that night was, this is far better," Jim compared. "And we hadn't thought to bring dinner. It was a spur of the moment idea."

Carolyn poured herself another glass of wine and noticed Jim was drinking coffee. A very talented someone was tickling the ivories on the baby grand at the pier. Carolyn heard herself tell Jim that she had been a failure at mastering the piano, a skill her Mother was convinced every educated woman should know. After eleven years of piano lessons, she had to admit that she was completely without any level of musical proficiency. Then she described her parents and her brother, Charles. She talked so long that she wondered if Jim was still there when she stopped. But they were in a boat. The wine.

"Could you kindly pour me some of that coffee?" Carolyn asked. "How are the brownies?"

"I was hoping you wouldn't ask so I could eat the last one," Jim teased.

Suddenly there were screams and applause from the hotel grounds. A new group of musicians was setting up on the bandstand. More screams and applause. "What's happening?" Carolyn asked.

"We're about to find out," Jim said, refilling his coffee cup. Then out of the night came a single long, clear, blast of a trumpet, followed by a quick crescendo of notes that bounced across the water like a Bourbon Street strut. More screams and applause! The rest of the musicians joined in and Carolyn recognized "West End Blues" performed like she'd never heard it before.

"It's Louis Armstrong! Well it's my lucky night," Jim exclaimed. I can't believe I get to see and hear him for free in Rosedale Beach. I couldn't afford to see him when I was living in New York City."

"You lived in New York City?" Carolyn asked.

"Yes, another one of my circles," Jim mumbled. Jim told Carolyn to sit steady because he wanted to move off the rowing seat to the boat bottom, so he could stretch out his long legs. By moving the ice chest forward, he lowered down and leaned back against his rowing seat, facing Carolyn. There, now he could look into her green eyes, even if he couldn't see them sparkle.

On the pavilion stage, Carolyn could make out four men and a woman, who was seated at the piano.

"They're "The Hot Five," and the pianist is Lil Hardin. Mr. Armstrong is the one with the trumpet," Jim noted. "He sure can make that horn talk."

The music was so smooth that conversation was taboo. Both Jim and Carolyn just wanted to listen. The boat rocked gently and the moon grew brighter as it rose in the sky. The Hot Five played "Ain't Misbehavin" and then " Heebie Jeebies" as screams and claps erupted each time the crowd recognized a new selection. Near the end of "Heebie Jeebies," Louis launched into scat, his gravelly voice rasping out the notes. "I can't tell what he's saying, but I like the beat," Jim exclaimed. "Makes me want to get up and dance."

Emotionally stirred, Carolyn leaned forward and grabbed Jim's hand. "Thank you for bringing me here tonight," she whispered. "The river is magical after dark, just like you said it might be. Thank you." She leaned forward even more to kiss his cheek, and stopped short when the boat pitched starboard. "Ooops, not a good idea," Carolyn said.

"It's a great idea," Jim laughed with her. "I'll see what I can do when we get ashore."

The row back to Oak Orchard was magical in the moonlight. Carolyn leaned back on her pillows and nearly dozed off from the rhythmic pull of Jim's rowing. Once Jim had the row boat securely grounded, he lifted Carolyn in his arms and carried her to shore, keeping her feet dry. Then he set her gently down on a picnic bench, raised her chin, and slowly kissed her on the mouth. Carolyn never felt more feminine, and she realized she would be seeing more of Jim Kelley.

CHAPTER TWELVE

One must stand a long time before a view to catch the relative living changes. These do not come at once.

- Jack Lewis

As much as they wished to see each other, Jim and Carolyn had precious little time to be together. Jim's Mosquito Control duties kept him busy even on many weekends, and Carolyn's after school field hockey team included Saturday scrimmages and practices. They had an understanding that they would speak over the phone on Sunday afternoons, but neither wanted to stay on the line too long, the phone being used primarily for emergencies or business.

At the kitchen table after Monday's dinner, Cora and Odette were huddled trying to choose the best bid they had received. It wasn't as easy as it seemed. Not all buyers offered a sale on the same terms.

Powell & Turner and Bill Vickers, two Ocean View buyers were offering 65 cents per pound "lumpus" or "clean house," meaning the entire flock, including any sick or damaged birds. Homer Pepper from Selbyville was offering 69 cents per pound "knots out," which meant he would only pay for healthy birds. Once Cora and Odette agreed on a buyer and signed the sale slip, both understood that the buyer had the right to determine "pick up" date. If the price for chicken was down, the buyer might wait as long as several weeks for the market to rise before pick-up. This would delay chicken house clean out for the next flock and mean fewer birds in the sale, since some were sure to die during the two week delay. The buyer had 'unknowns' too, since some birds would die in truck transport to the Philadelphia processing plants. Cora intensified her prayers that "the good Lord" would provide optimal conditions of high market prices and a swift pick up.

"I hear Jack Udell of Eagle Poultry is hoping to get enough capital together to build a dressing plant in Frankford," Cora was sighing. "Wouldn't that make things so much easier?"

"Wouldn't it now!" Odette agreed.

"At least we now have lots of local choices for mash, bags, biddies, and antibiotics. Things in the industry are changing so fast, that I can barely keep up," Cora talked on, giving her mind time to make the all-important decision. Finally she signed the sale agreement from Homer Pepper of Selbyville, at the higher rate, for healthy birds only. Since Bill Vickers from Ocean View was related to Cora by marriage, she realized she might be sorry later. But business was business.

Three days later at dinnertime, Cora received a phone call that the catching crew would arrive at 3:00 a.m. Cora praised God that her prayers had been answered. Odette, too excited to sleep, took a shower at midnight, fixed herself a BLT and paced the floor. When Carolyn awoke and descended the apartment steps to her usual perch, the chickens were almost loaded. Four black males worked in pairs to "snatch" the birds and place them into wooden crates, or coops. A Pepper Poultry truck sat just outside the door of the chicken house and had coops stacked to its ceiling.

Even though she wanted to congratulate Odette, Carolyn headed off to school. She could see that Odette was deep in discussion with the crew chief. The point of contention was the number of birds that had been set aside as "sickly" or "damaged." Occasionally a bird's neck would get snapped in the catching process, and it was limply added to the "inferior" group. Since local practice allowed catchers to take home badly bruised or killed carcasses, Odette watched like a hawk to make sure there was no intentional maiming. Even though the percentage of "knots out" was not great, Odette did her duty to challenge many of the designations. The back and forth banter was expected and made the catchers and crew chief respect Odette's knowledge before the crucial weighing out. Once all the coops were filled and loaded, each truck was weighed a second time. The difference determined the total pounds to be paid at the .69 cent price. Odette calculated each weighing and triple checked her math. She brooded like a mother hen over her flock, being aware of the spots where exactness mattered. Both buyer and seller "trusted" but "verified" since breeders had been known to put gravel into the mash before pick up. But Odette knew that Cora had selected Homer Pepper because his reputation and word were highly trusted.

About mid-morning, halfway through her second period English class, Carolyn had an uneasy feeling in the pit of her stomach. She almost gasped aloud when she realized she hadn't given a thought to her feathered friend with the red string around his ankle. How tragic! What an uncaring soul she was! At lunchtime, she dashed for the school office and asked to use the phone, saying it was an emergency. No one answered at the farmhouse, and Carolyn spent the rest of the afternoon trying not to think about the insides of a dressing plant.

Carolyn was unusually quiet at dinner, and she was too embarrassed to confess the cause of her "blues" when Cora inquired, "What's wrong dear?" Even George was noticeably cheery as Odette and Cora celebrated the morning sale. Cora said she would have time in a few days to pay the outstanding bills and calculate their true profit. Then she and Odette could decide how much to invest in the next breeding cycle, after the poultry house was scraped out and redressed with clean wood shavings. Carolyn could hardly believe that the chickens were gone and that the whole process would start all over. She dashed up the apartment steps, not wanting to even look down the empty bay from her favorite step.

When Carolyn opened her bedroom door, a "Cluck-cl-cl-cluck" sound greeted her. There in the center of her rug, was a chicken coop holding her red string friend. Carolyn squealed and lifted him up into her arms in delight. "Now I guess I'm going to have to give you a name," Carolyn said, swiveling around to find Odette beaming in the doorway.

"I set him aside for you before the catchers arrived. I thought you might want to keep him for a while, or say a proper "good bye."

"OH, Odette, thank you so, so much! I know it's silly and immature, but the thought of him being gassed and de-feathered right now is just too heartbreaking. You are a true friend," Carolyn gushed, hugging Odette.

"Don't ask me what we're going to do with him now. You can be darn sure no chicken is going to share my apartment," Odette exclaimed, as the two giggled.

At C.C.C. Company 1224 in Lewes, mosquito control measures continued on schedule, but Jim's heart and mind were on Carolyn. He could see that the lady was not ready for a serious relationship and that her students and her new surroundings were the things captivating her soul. Jim knew he was madly in love with Carolyn, but felt relieved that there was still time for him to become more financially secure, if that was possible in these uncertain times.

"That's a beautiful painting. Whose house is it?"

Jim asked as he viewed the completed canvas in Jack Lewis' newly assigned art space.

"Don't you recognize it?" Jack teased. "You're not the only one who can 'kiss up to the brass.' You are looking at the home of Colonel Wilbur S. Corkran and Louise Chambers Corkran, named "The Homestead" in Rehoboth. I've been working on it all week, and I'm hoping it will please Mrs. Corkran in every way."

"You don't say," Jim muttered, trying not to sound too impressed.

"Yes, I do say. Mrs. Corkran brought me out a cup of tea while I was sketching in her front yard, and she asked me if I thought Rehoboth would support an Art League. We had quite a lovely conversation," Jack's eyes twinkled, rubbing it in.

Jack had made many sketches of the Lewes Camp buildings since his arrival. Jim especially liked the one of the prize winning barracks in their recent garden competition where Jack had masterfully captured the roses and bright summer flowers around the winning barracks doorstep. Jim thought the sketch was a beautiful record of the esprit de corps and pride the men took in their C.C.C. living quarters.

"I think I'll do that one in oils," Jack shared, looking at the winning barracks sketch.

"What's this over here?" Jim questioned, looking at a mucky substance piled on newspapers.

"Oh, that. I'm testing composites trying to find the best mixture to make facemasks."

"Facemasks?"

"Yes, I'm working with some of the boys on a stage

production, and making our own costume parts helps keep the costs down. Got to stay within the allotted budget, you know."

"Didn't realize after-dinner entertainment was in your job description," Jim mused.

"It's called 'cultural arts,' and yes, I'm the designated ring leader of all those willing to share their talents and nerve. I enjoy the challenge."

"So let me guess. This mushy stuff on the table came from the salt marsh or some riverbed within walking distance. Right?"

"Right, indeed. Once I mix the clay with a little newspaper mash, I think the substance will be perfect to form marionettes. Folks are less reserved when they speak through a surrogate, and I've found that marionettes make for great productions," Jack explained.

Masks, marionettes, Jim shook his head, and wondered what else Jack knew how to do. "Say, would you be interested in going to dinner at a friend of mine's house this Sunday? Jim asked.

"Sure, I never turn down a home cooked meal."

"Great."

As he walked back to his Foreman's desk, Jim found himself smiling and was truly happy artist Jack Lewis had been assigned time in Lewes. His paintings, plays, and philosophies were becoming a welcome diversion from the drudgery of digging ditches.

Painting "Prize Winning Barracks" by C.C.C. artist Jack Lewis, 1936 oil on canvas, with permission from the U. S. National Archives and Records Administration and the Delaware Division of Historical and Cultural Affairs.

CHAPTER THIRTEEN

One need not travel over the geographical world to discover its glories. He need merely to see it on an early morning or at dusk. Should he rise with the sun, he will see his usual world transformed in the wonder of a soft, liquid light of embryonic day.
- Jack Lewis

About nine in the morning, the Officer of the Day came hurriedly to Jim's desk, saying, "Sergeant Kelley, Jack Lewis needs your help."

"Sure, is he in his art studio?" Jim responded, barely looking up.

"No sir. He just phoned into the duty post to say that he needs you to come to the Slaughter Beach Police Station." Jim's head snapped to attention. "He said for you to wear your hat and look as official as possible."

"Did he say anything else, Officer?"

"He just asked that you not let the paint get dry. Does that mean anything?"

Jim tried to keep a straight face, and with a deep, regimented voice said, "Please phone the Police Station back and let them know I'm on my way. Thank you."

When Jim entered the Slaughter Beach Station, he could see Jack seated behind the bars of the holding area. At least he wasn't in handcuffs. "Hello, I'm Sergeant Kelley from Company 1224 in Lewes, and I've come to assist Jack Lewis. What seems to be the problem?"

"I'm Corporal Layton, the Troop Commander here, and Mr. Lewis is being held for suspicious behavior on state marshlands. Our night patrolman found him walking in the dark and trailed him from the road into the marsh for about a mile. Then he watched Mr. Lewis make drawings of the canals and inlets."

Corporal Layton paused, so Jim realized a reaction was called for.

"Yes, I am sure that is exactly what Mr. Lewis was doing. Jack Lewis is an artist working under the direction of Colonel W.S. Corkran, Superintendent of the Delaware Mosquito Control Commission. Mr. Lewis' art provides a concrete record of the work of our corpsmen."

"Do you expect me to believe that?" Corporal Layton replied with a straight face, to Jim's disbelief.

"Yes sir, I implore you to believe it because it's the

truth."

"Could I please see some identification and I need a phone number for Col. Corkran," Corporal Layton demanded, very seriously.

"Yes, indeed," Jim said quickly, pulling out his Army Reserve and C.C.C. credentials. He also placed a copy of Jack's assignment papers on the desk, thankful that he had grabbed them before leaving post.

Officer Layton read each paper very slowly and carefully and then asked the only other policeman present to read them as well. "Will you verify in writing that this man, Jack Lewis, is who you say he is?"

"Most certainly", Jim answered. Corporal Layton then produced an incident report form that had been partially completed, and pointed to the space for Jim's statement and signature.

"You understand, Sergeant Kelley, that by signing you are legally responsible for the truth of your affidavit."

"Yes, I fully understand," Jim replied and cynically thought that perhaps he should stand and salute for full effect.

"Now you and Mr. Lewis may leave, but we will be keeping the roll of film from his camera," Corporal Layton directed. "He can take his sketch pad, pen, and camera back now," Officer Layton said, handing Jim the three items."

"A camera? You were taking pictures?" Jim inquired sternly when the two men were back inside the truck. "And how did you get all the way up here before daylight?"

"I knew it was going to be a glorious sunrise, and at three-thirty when I couldn't sleep, I grabbed my camera to catch the early morning light. A sketch doesn't capture the embryonic liquid of the first rays. I hitched a ride on a Lewes Dairy Truck that was headed north, and the rest is history, regrettably," Jack explained. "I had no idea anyone would be interested in what I was doing so early."

"Well from now on, if you leave post before daybreak, please sign out with the Duty Officer. I know you were just doing your job, but ......boy, those guys were on edge!" Jim reflected. "What kinds of questions did they ask you?"

"They kept asking me why I was drawing in the marsh, and they wanted to know who I would give my photos to. My answers just didn't satisfy them because they asked me the same questions six times," Jack recounted. "Thanks, buddy, for coming to my rescue. It was uncomfortable in there."

"You're welcome, but if this incident generates another letter of reprimand from Col. Corkran, you are in for it!" Jim threatened. "Never a dull moment in mosquito control."

Sunday thankfully came without any fallout from Jack's arrest, and the two men were again walking to town. "Where is it we are headed after church?" Jack asked.

"To my friend Hannah Marshall's house for dinner, and perhaps even for some tennis. They have a clay court on the grounds of their mansion "Gray Gables." Hannah has two sisters, Louise and Helen, and a couple brothers I haven't met. I thought you would enjoy the female company, and of course Mrs. Marshall's fabulous food," Jim explained.

Walking was the usual mode of transportation as Jim and Jack hiked from Camp MC-51 to downtown Lewes for Sunday church services. The November air was brisk and the two men were striding at an energetic pace to keep warm. Each time they passed one of Lewes' historic landmarks, Jim would enthusiastically explain its significance to Jack. The Ryves Holt House, the Maull House, the Rabbit's Ferry House, the Cannonball House, the Burton-Ingram House, the Lewes Presbyterian Church, St. Peter's Episcopal Church---Jim had read, and was able to remember, why each was important, and he took delight in sharing the history.

"Now which one of these gals are you sweet on, so I can steer clear?" Jack asked.

Jim sighed, and paused some more, and then said, "Hannah and I have had some fun together the last two years, but…..well…"

"Well what?"

"I've met someone else who I just can't stop thinking about. She's a teacher at the Selbyville School and she's quite captivating. I feel a little guilty even accepting Hannah's invitation and I'm dreading telling her things will be different between us from now on."

"Oh, I do love those 'I've met someone else' moments," Jack's eyes sparkled. "They are never pleasant, but always character building. Good luck with that, my man."

Jim grimaced and said, "Jack, you might have met Hannah's sister, Louise, when you visited Colonel Corkran. She's one of his two office Secretaries. I'm indebted to her because she's been putting in some good words about me to the Colonel. Remember I told you I'd received a letter of reprimand from him last year?"

"Well what do you think Louise will tell the Colonel when you dump her sister?" Jack snipped, ever quick to hit upon the crux of the situation.

"You get right to the point, don't you?" Jim smiled. "I'm going to pray in church this morning that I find just the right words for Hannah, and that providence will provide mercy from Louise. I know that's asking a lot."

"Well, I'll pray on the matter too, and I'm sure God will hear one of us," Jack advised. "Let's plan to meet at the Zwaannendael Museum in an hour. My Episcopal service is standard format and will not exceed that. If your Methodist preacher man goes overboard, just duck out because I don't want to have time to do a painting waiting for you."

"I way outrank you, and you show me no respect," Jim parlayed as they parted company. Jim went inside Bethel United Methodist church as Jack quickened his pace to worship at historic St. Peter's Episcopal.

They had a feast at Gray Gables and the Marshall family showed them every kindness. Jack was a hit with all the females, and he swung a tennis racket like he'd been on the courts since infancy. Extra-long arms and legs were a decided advantage to Jack, but his skill

158

was due to more than physique. Ever the gentleman, Jack could place the tennis ball wherever he wanted, and he treated every opponent kindly, even Jim.

"So how long have you been playing tennis?" Jim asked on the walk home. The moon had not risen, and it was quite dark as the two men walked Kings Highway, and then east on Savannah Road.

"For as long as I can remember. I was Captain of my high school team, and I played some matches at Rutgers," Jack continued. "Did you have that talk with Hannah?"

"Regrettably, yes, while you were volleying against Louise and Helen. No words are the 'right words,' and after you've said them, there isn't nearly as much left to talk about. I just told her the truth--- that I had met someone else, and that I would always remember the fun we had together. She kept smiling, but the light went out of her eyes right after I spoke those words, and I felt like a cad. But hinting around, or not saying anything, would have been much crueler, don't you think?"

"Are you sure she wasn't relieved to be rid of you?" Jack said smartly.

Jim laughed in spite of feeling miserable. No response was needed, and the two men enjoyed the peaceful darkness in silence until they reached camp.

Back in Selbyville, Carolyn spent Sunday evening confessing in writing to Virginia that she had recently met a man who interested her.

Quillen's Farm
RD #2

Selbyville, Delaware

Dear Virginia,

Where do the months go? Can you believe we're finishing our first year as teachers? A year ago, I tried to envision what it would be like. Well my imaginings didn't come close to reality, and I positively love what I'm doing. How is it going with you? I know we are both so-oo-oo busy, but I love your letters. Send more.

I must confess that I've been holding out on you about one part of my new life. A few months ago I met a man named Jim Kelley who works with the State of Delaware's Mosquito Control corps. He's also in the Army Reserves, and he's had other varied life experiences that I'm still learning about, in Idaho, New York City, and Philadelphia. I just realized that I don't know how old he is, but he must be at least five years older than I am. Anyway, what's most important is that he seems like a very sweet man. And of course he's 6'2" with blonde hair, blue eyes, very white teeth, and freckles---making for a 'Grade A' composite.

Has Bob popped the question, or do you two just want to enjoy the uncomplicated life a while longer? Please tell me what your English classes are studying now and describe your Pottstown High classroom for me. I'm envious that you have juniors and seniors, and I have only ninth graders.

My basketball team had a tremendously good season, with only two defeats. We finished first at the Sussex County Play Day, and my Selbyville team was awarded the "most improved" certificate. I am so proud of the way the girls have "bonded" this year to strengthen both our offense and defense. I'm not coaching now, but I'm enjoying the softball, tennis, and track in my physical education classes. I can't wait for the warm weather to return. You know, the hotter the better for me.

My roommate, Odette Wright, has successfully raised two broods of chickens while completing courses at Delaware State College. You have no idea the work involved with mothering 12,000 chickens! I'll explain when we get together, hopefully in May, after both our semesters end. Are you planning on being back in Philadelphia then? We simply must get some time together.

Must run. Miss you so much.
Sincerely, Carolyn

Late Monday afternoon, Odette and Carolyn were sharing the work table in their kitchen-living area. Carolyn was busy proofing a paper Odette had to write for her Education Fundamentals class, while Odette focused on making them meat loaf sandwiches.

"My brother, Leonard, says something is going on at the Cape," Odette said, spreading thick the mayonnaise.

"Cape Henlopen?" Carolyn verified.

"Yes, there's unusual boat activity that everyone is 'hush hush' about. Leonard doesn't yet know why all the commotion, but he'll find out soon.

"Maybe I'll ask Sergeant Kelley if he's seen anything unusual in Lewes. That's right at Cape Henlopen.   If I learn anything, I'll be sure to tell you so you can let Leonard know.

"Thanks," Odette said, looking a bit skeptical.

CHAPTER FOURTEEN

There should be a dance for the purpose of recording all the beautiful little movements, the beauty in all the commonplace little things of life.

- Jack Lewis

Jim became increasingly worried about Rocco. His letters had suddenly ceased, after coming with weekly regularity for a year. Rocco Zarrillo could type a letter so fast that Jim was sure something must be wrong. Hating to admit the severity of his concerns, Jim wrote a letter of inquiry to the C.C.C. Camp Superintendent in Arroyo Grande, California.

Jack Lewis' artistic endeavors were helping keep Jim's mind off Rocco. A few nights before, Jack's troupe presented "The Shooting of Dan McGrew" and the classic Italian Opera "Pagliacci." Leave it to Jack to believe he could use young and naïve C.C.C.

recruits to bring to life "the vengeance of spurned love" as portrayed by clowns in an opera and cowboys in a saloon. And *believe* he did! Jim recognized the colorful clown masks as the artistic products of the soggy heap of clay on Jack's work table. To Jim's constant amazement, Jack's cultural ploys always engendered shouts of joy and applause. But Italian opera, that took guts.

Recognizing how much Jim loved the theater, Jack sometimes asked Jim to be present during dress rehearsals. The two men swapped critiques of shows they both had seen in Philadelphia and New York City. Next Saturday night, "The Strolling Marionettes," Jack's thespians, were performing a three act show on the stage of Hotel Caesar Rodney in Lewes. The larger venue allowed more people to attend, including women, who as members of the cast and the audience attracted as many of the C.C.C. boys who could get the night off-post.

Jim attended the only dress rehearsal, and was in awe that Jack pulled it together so artfully, especially given his meager budget and his limited time with the cast of volunteers. Act I was the "Ransom of Red Chief," a play adapted from O. Henry's short story about a kidnapping that went badly. It had only three actors, including the Horn sisters who were not novices to the stage.

During Act II "Lust For Treasure," Jim marveled at the way Jack employed marionettes to tell about the sinking of the ship DeBraak in the Lewes harbor and the subsequent search for its contents. "Lust

For Treasure's" six characters were marionettes that had strings attached to their arms and legs and were manipulated from above by six cast members. Jack was not kidding when he told Jim he "liked marionettes." Six additional cast members provided the voices for the marionettes as they jerkily "spoke" the lines Jim was sure Jack had written.

Act III, "Sorcerer's Apprentice" was a pantomime of a symphonic poem by the French composer Paul Dukas. Jim chuckled as an apprentice imitates his master, the sorcerer, and manages to bring a broom to life. The broom goes out of control and the apprentice forgets the magic words to calm it. Jim thought the comedy a bit convoluted, but Jack's marionettes made the humor easy to follow. Jim gave all three acts a "thumbs up" for entertainment and education.

Once a year, all four of the Mosquito Control C.C.C. camps met in Leipsic, Delaware for a Field Day. Jim and Jack, who were riding in the cab of a half-ton, were anticipating both the barbeque and the camaraderie of the afternoon's games. Last year there had been baseball, tug-of-war, and ditch digging to see which company could cut the most sod in ten minutes.

"Have you had any word from Rocco?" Jack inquired.

"No, not a thing."

"Well, no news is good news. He's probably headed to the California version of our field day right now. What a beautiful day for a gathering of the Corps."

"Did the Colonel ask you to prepare any entertainment?" Jim inquired.

"No, I got the day off, but I do have my accordion in the back of the truck. Did you hear what the Colonel wants us to do at the Harrington State Fair in July?" Jack asked.

"No, but I thought it was great public relations last year when you dressed the guys as mosquitos and had them "exterminated," Jim chuckled.

"In addition to our float, Col. Corkran wants me to make ten masks for common occupations like 'butcher,' 'baker,' 'farmer,' etc. and have the costumed men stroll around the Fair Grounds singing the praises of the C.C.C.," Jack illuminated. "Mind you, it's guaranteed to be 100 degrees in the shade and my masks might melt, but we're going through with it anyway."

"Anything to keep the boss happy. The Colonel sure is a go-getter," Jim spoke from experience. "What's the theme for our float this year?"

"It will be the usual marsh scene with sod and grasses. But we've been told to emphasize "careful layout of ditches" since there's been complaints from businessmen that the oysters and the muskrats are hurt by our drainage efforts. So we'll put a couple surveyors with equipment on our float too. Doesn't that beat all?"

"Well, the State Fair is a political event, not just a gathering of farmers. Remember the Colonel has to please Governor Buck, and the Fair is the Governor's showcase," Jim mused. "And understand that the Governor is not one to mess with. In 1933, Governor Buck temporarily dissolved the Legislature to resolve a funding dispute...Say, did you remember to grab the

C.C.C. Flag to plant on top of the sod mountain after the games?"

"Sure did. And I know just the corpsman to shimmy to the top to do the honors. I'll get him lined up," Jack offered. "*The Delaware State News* will want that photo."

"This might be my last Field Day," Jim shared.

"What? You aren't leaving us, are you?" asked Jack.

"The Forestry Service has authorized a new C.C.C. Company at Redden Forest. Since I have experience in soil conservation from Idaho, I've been transferred to lay-out and help run the new Camp S-53. We will be planting a lot of trees, and it will be nice to have a break from digging ditches," Jim sighed. "I'm now classified as a 'Local Experienced Man,' which sounds quite impressive, don't you think?"

For once, Jack was quiet.

At the end of the day, after the Magnolia boys had claimed bragging rights as winners of the most events, everyone gathered around the sod mountain adorned with the Conservation Corps Flag. Colonel Corkran made a speech and then one of the men from MC-54, with apologies to President Lincoln, read *The Magnolia Address*:

Eight months and six days ago, our predecessors brought forth from this apple orchard a new encampment, conceived by Roosevelt and dedicated to the proposition of getting rid of mosquitoes.

We are now engaged in a great civil strife, testing whether this spade or any spade so constructed, or so leaned upon, can long endure.

We are sunk into a great marsh land in Delaware, providing a final resting place for all forbears of the mosquito that the tourists and townspeople might sleep in peace.

It is altogether fitting and proper that we should do this. But in a larger nonsense, we cannot excavate, we cannot irrigate, we cannot hollow this ground. The "goldbrickers" present and absent who struggle here have driven us far beyond our poor power of patience to remonstrate with them. The world will little note nor long remember what we say to them, but it can never forget what they didn't do here.

It is for us, the remainder, rather to be excavating here on the unfinished work which they who struggled here have thus far so nobly deserted. It is rather for them not to be here, rather than engage in unintentional labor, that from these "goldbrickers" we take decreased emotion to that cause to which they gave their last full measure of devotion: that we highly resolve that these mosquitoes shall breed, but not here, that this camp shall have a new freedom from bites; and that discipline of the Army, by the Army and for the CCC shall not perish for the lack of relief.

History lover Jim, who idolized Abraham Lincoln since boyhood, thought it had been a memorable day. As he maneuvered the half-ton truck loaded to the max, he smiled at the sound of Jack's accordion and the chorus of male voices echoing from the flatbed behind him.

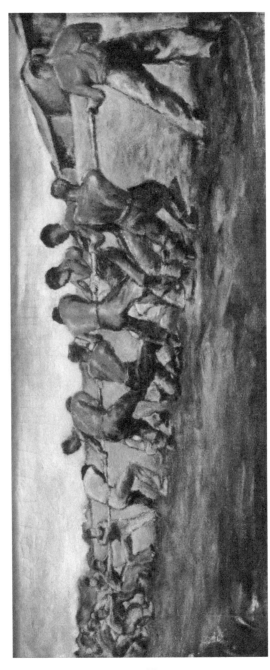

Painting "Tug of War" by C.C.C. artist Jack Lewis, 1936 oil on canvas, with permission from the U.S. National Archives and Records Adminstration and the Delaware Division of Historical and Cultural Affairs.

CHAPTER FIFTEEN

There is a naturalness about small town curiosity that is far stronger and wiser than the wisdom of the city dweller.

- Jack Lewis

Carolyn and Jim were making holly wreaths at the Quillen farm late on a Saturday afternoon. Cora had gathered a group of willing workers, all enticed by Cora's dinner offer that included her famous peach pie. The goal was to make as many eight inch wreaths as they could with the holly, pine, and cedar that George and his farm hand had cut. They would be paid eight cents for each wreath. Cora had calculated their earnings would be greater if they didn't make any of the larger twelve inch wreaths, which brought two more cents, but took a lot more greens.

"Ouch! I can feel the prickle through my gloves," Carolyn complained, still working on just her second wreath. "Cora, I don't see how you do it so fast. And your finished product is beautiful, unlike mine that looks like it's been stomped on," she mumbled, holding it up for all to see.

"I've had a lot of years of practice trying to make my wreaths look better than ones made by Norman Justice in Ocean View. People come from all around just to buy his wreaths. Rumor has it that he's talked the buyer from Milton into paying him two cents more." Carolyn noticed that Cora had taken Carolyn's last creation off the wreath stand and was sprucing it up.

Weekends were a blissful oasis in a frantic work week for Jim and Carolyn. They both longed for Saturday, or Sunday, or occasionally both days, to be together. The Lewes C.C.C. Camp was no place for Carolyn, so more often than not, they met at the farm. After dinner they might drive to a friend's house, or to see a movie at the Clayton in Dagsboro. Jim was in heaven when he was with Carolyn, and his smile never stopped. Although today, Carolyn noticed that he was quieter than usual. When they took a water break, Carolyn asked him if anything was wrong?

"I'm so terribly worried about my friend Rocco Zarrillo. There have been no letters for months now, and my written inquiries have produced no new information. I'm very discouraged, and extremely fearful that something bad has happened to him."

"You don't suppose he just moved on with his life?" Carolyn asked, and then wished she hadn't, when she saw the expression on Jim's face.

"I wish I could believe that because then I'd know

he's ok," Jim replied. "But I don't….believe that."

"Waiting is the hardest part of life," Lillian White chimed in. "Please forgive me for overhearing, but like the Twenty-Seventh Psalm says, 'Be strong and take heart, and wait on the Lord'. Life has taught me that God gives a good answer in *his* time. But waiting on the Lord is most difficult." Jim shook his head resolutely, wanting to agree with Lillian.

Lillian was Cora's best friend from Bethel Mariner's Church in Ocean View. Carolyn loved the inflection of Lillian's British accent. During the Great War, Lillian met her American husband- to-be while dancing at Blackpool. Carolyn thought Lillian was as beautiful and as sophisticated as any Philadelphia debutante she had ever met, but Carolyn was a bit surprised that Lillian was so well versed in the Bible. Oh well, Sussex County life was turning out to be anything but predictable.

"I'd say we have our first stand half-full," Jim calculated. Wreath stands were upright poles attached to two crossed boards, or feet that held forty to fifty stacked-up wreaths.

"For our next stand, let's wind some Creeping Jenny into each one," Odette suggested. Who has more red berries? I'm just about out."

"Here are some berries, Odette, but let me have some of your pine cones," Carolyn replied. "Oh, Odette, tell Jim what Leonard told you about the water activity near the Cape."

Odette looked up with surprise and then said that Leonard had mentioned something in passing about unusual boat activity near the mouth of the Bay. Carolyn could see that Odette didn't want to talk about it, especially to Jim.

"Well, I had an unusual event myself," Jim replied. "One of my men was arrested by the Slaughter Beach Police, and when I went to identify him, I was astounded by the wary attitude of the local authorities. They all but said they thought my man was a spy, and they made me sign an affidavit attesting to his identity."

"Perhaps they thought he was an escaped convict or something," Odette offered, to Carolyn's raised eyebrow. "Times are tough, and financial stress can make people do crazy things," Odette explained, while Carolyn wondered about the sudden downplay of Leonard's distress signal.

As Carolyn's fingers wrestled with the greens, her mind deftly rehashed some recent changes. She thought of several of her students who had such potential for thinking and expressing themselves in writing. Billy Walker was one of them, and she imagined him becoming an accomplished lawyer or Delaware's Attorney General someday. But her heart ached because she saw evidence that his family was struggling to make ends meet. Billy often lacked pencils and school supplies, and Carolyn didn't hold out much hope that when the time came for college he would have the resources and freedom from guilt to leave home.

Carolyn also reflected on Jim's new work assignment, that he had enthusiastically described to her. Redden State Forest Camp S-53, was completed in record time. C.C.C. men, Forestry Department personnel, and U.S. Army men built fourteen buildings within two months. For Jim, it was the third time he had helped set up a Civilian Conservation Corps camp, and he was very pleased with the preparation of the grounds and the quality of the new construction. 185 Veterans in C.C.C. Company 2210 from Montpelier, Vermont were joined by Company 1293 from Fort Dix, New Jersey. Jim liked the management style of young First Lieutenant Thayer Royal, of Holden Massachusetts, who was in charge of the Vermont Company. Learning over two hundred new names and hearing their stories was a challenge Jim never tired of, and that made him a good supervisor. But he did miss some of his mosquito control friends, especially Jack Lewis.

The wreath makers worked until it got too dark to see. Around the dinner table they discussed Jim's new assignment, Carolyn's basketball prospects, Odette's new brood, and everyone exclaimed that Cora's peach pie was scrumptious, as usual, even if the peaches had been frozen from last July. Carolyn could see that Jim was tired from the week's activities, and she pleaded with him to leave right after dinner so he would stay awake on the drive alone back to Redden. Jim thought it was a sure sign that she loved him, even though he had learned that Carolyn was not ever one to verbalize it.

CHAPTER SIXTEEN

*We must realize that every touch
of the brush must touch the heart
and mind of the painter.*
- Jack Lewis

Jim and his work crew were nearly finished stacking huge piles of marsh grass that towered above their heads. They had been at it all day, and Jim's lower back was aching. As a Forestry Supervisor, he hadn't done a lot of slinging the pitchfork, but his back hurt anyway. The cooler weather made Jim less concerned about the twenty huge stacks of grass catching fire. Once the grass "seasoned," it could be sold for farm feed. But while Mother Nature did her thing, fire was a constant hazard.

In 1930, Delaware's largest forest area, the Great Cypress Swamp between Gumboro and Selbyville caught fire and burned for days, destroying 30,000 acres of forested swampland. The terrible event caused fire towers to be built and forest wardens to be hired by the State. William Taber, the State Forester, was charged with making sure Delaware forests never again went up in flames.

Jim now had three big bosses to report to----the State Forester Taber, Colonel Grant of the U. S. Army, and Col. Corkran of the C.C.C. While there was a lot of paperwork for Jim, he was amazed that the three governmental agencies collaborated so smoothly. The C.C.C. men provided the labor, the Army provided equipment and administrative support, and the State and National Forest Service set the agenda for work projects focused on timber production, outdoor recreation, and wildlife conservation. The work was a lot more diversified than it had been in mosquito control. Jim often found himself planting trees, constructing roads, building picnic pavilions and picnic tables, clearing walking trails, creating fire breaks and digging ditches to prevent forest fires.

As the months rolled by, Jim was engrossed in his job and even more in love with Carolyn. His work kept him occupied every minute, but that didn't keep his mind from focusing on the future. Meeting Carolyn had changed everything. He still felt like he was treading water because college wasn't even on the radar screen. Jim knew that the money he was sending home to Delmar each month was crucial for his family. But Jim's heart and mind longed to return to college, and he realized he needed to finish his Bachelor's Degree to make anything of himself. The uncertainty of the times was weighing heavily on his mind.

In July Jim's world came crashing down one ordinary afternoon when he retrieved his mail.

United States Department of Agriculture
Forest Service
Coeur D'Alene National Forest, Idaho

July 11, 1936
Dear Friend:

In answer to your letter of June 3, 1936, I am sorry to say that Rocco Zarrillo died about the 10th day of April.

He worked for me during the summer months of 1935 as a C.C.C. Leader. I promoted him to Sub-Foreman about October 20 and he was transferred to F-132 Co. 531 at Prichard, Idaho. The Superintendent's name was Gordon Valentine. During this time Rocco made friends with everyone he came in contact with and was doing excellent work as a Forestry Service Foreman.

About the 20 of March while working on the job, a rolling rock struck his hand resulting in the amputation of a finger. While he was in the hospital he developed pneumonia which caused his death. I saw him at the hospital about five days before his death and he was feeling fine and was in the best of spirits. He thought he would be back on the job soon. He took a set-back shortly after that and didn't last long. He was the picture of health and had the best medical care during his short illness.

Words cannot express my feelings towards

Rocco. Although I only knew him about ten months, he was one of my best friends. He was a gentleman if there ever was one.

I do not know his parents' address but maybe I could find out through the Forest Service. If I can give you any other information, I would be only too glad to do so.

Your friend,
Lyle Brown
Route 2
Coeur D'Alene, Idaho

P.S. The body was sent east to his parents.

Jim was devastated. The letter, and another that came later, confirmed his worst fears. It seemed impossible that someone as young and as full of life as Rocco was gone. Jim withdrew into himself and at first adopted a stoic attitude, much like he had done when he was forced to drop out of Randolph Macon. On automatic pilot, he emotionlessly performed the days duties, pretending nothing was different. But underneath, he was seething with anger, sadness, regret, and even guilt that he had sent Rocco westward. He didn't know how or why Rocco moved from California back to Idaho, and Jim couldn't fathom how someone could die so quickly just from the loss of a finger. Not that those details mattered now.

Jim didn't communicate with Carolyn for two weeks. He knew he was in a horrible state, and he just wasn't up to telling her the bad news. Somehow

Rocco's death reinforced his lack of control over the important things in his life.

Carolyn was working the summer at Camp Otonka, a girls' camp on Vines Creek near Millsboro. After Jim didn't come to see her on two consecutive Saturdays, she became increasingly concerned. Finally, Carolyn received a short note from Jim conveying the news of Rocco's death. Jim's normally beautiful handwriting was splashed sloppily across the page. The note was formal and to the point, written in Army language. It didn't sound like Jim at all.

The following Sunday, Carolyn took action. She drove her Buick to Redden State Forest, and told the sentry at the camp entrance that she wanted to speak to Jim. Carolyn waited for what seemed like an eternity, until Jim finally strode toward her car.

"Well, this is certainly a surprise," Jim greeted her, opening the car door and slipping into the passenger seat. He leaned over and gave her a quick kiss. Carolyn could see the bags under Jim's eyes and the exhausted slope of his shoulders. He looked like he hadn't slept for days.

Carolyn waited a moment, and then began cautiously, "I am so very, very sorry about Rocco. How I wish the letter had contained better news. It's just so sad."

Jim was silent. After a long pause, his lower lip trembled, and he whispered, "Yes, we had gone through so many good and bad times together… Rocco was so full of life, and so young…." Then the tears started to spill down Jim's cheeks, and he put his head into his hands and sobbed softly.

Carolyn waited and waited and just let him cry. Then she put her hand over his, drew it to her mouth, and kissed it. Next she reached into the Buick glove compartment and found a hankie and gave it to Jim. He blew his nose, and raised his head to look into her eyes for the first time since he opened the car door.

"Well, I guess I needed that," Jim said apologetically. "Miraculously, I do feel better. The last two weeks have been terrible. I just haven't been able to put Rocco out of my mind."

"Grief is a natural process," Carolyn counseled, "and crying is good for the soul. Do you have a minute so we could try out one of those hiking trails your men have been clearing? I'd really like a walk through the woods right now."

Jim and Carolyn walked hand in hand into the shady recesses of Redden Forest. The pines and holly trees provided coolness on a late July afternoon and before long Jim was identifying plants and flowers and birds. Carolyn smiled as she saw him take joy in the instruction. Jim really was a teacher at heart.

Perhaps it was the stress of Rocco's death, but Jim grew much more relaxed than Carolyn had ever seen him   He chatted away, making up for the stoic silence of the past two weeks. "I really like my duties here at Redden," Jim shared. "There's such a variety of tasks that I haven't tired of them yet. And the two units of boys we've been sent this time are the best I've worked with."

"Then you think you want to be a Forester forever?"

Carolyn asked.

"No, I don't think so. I very much want to finish college. And one day, the Civilian Conservation Corps will disband. It's inevitable. I have to find a way to work my way back into school."

"You really think Roosevelt will let the Corps die?" Carolyn asked dubiously.

"Yes, nothing lasts forever. And the way things are going in Europe, our country's resources could be allocated to priorities other than soil conservation. But it's all so uncertain. I wish I had a crystal ball to tell me where my life is headed," Jim pondered, uncharacteristically sharing his thoughts.

"Well, I'm proud of the path you have taken so far," Carolyn said, giving Jim her brightest smile. 'If life was scripted, we would all be bored," Carolyn quipped, remembering the reason she took her teaching job in Selbyville. "Maybe we should be thankful for the uncertainty of the times? It keeps us on our toes."

Jim laughed, not entirely convinced of her logic. But Jim was amazed that a brief hour and a half with Carolyn had soothed his anger and resentment. He slept blissfully that night for the first time in weeks.

CHAPTER SEVENTEEN

Wonder is infinite in the natural order of the universe; the only requisite is that one wants it, and he will find it to the extent of his desire.

- Jack Lewis

Jim's transfer to Ft. DuPont in Delaware City was a blessing and a curse for Jim and Carolyn. Now separated by a two hour drive, they had to exchange letters to continue their relationship. Jim's handwriting was beautifully scripted and his letters read like poetry. Carolyn's handwriting was tiny and she often wrote in stream of consciousness phrases that were challenging to decipher, even for Jim who loved her very much and was willing to put in the extra effort.

The long distance phone charge from Sussex County to New Castle County made letter writing mandatory, so both Carolyn and Jim found time in their programmed work week to write one or two letters. In a way, the separation forced them to say things to each other that might have gone unsaid if they had seen each other daily.

When he left Redden State Forest, Jim was emotionally "down," about leaving Carolyn and about Rocco's death. But early on in their letter exchange, Carolyn saw that Jim's outlook was more up-beat than she ever imagined it could be. Excitedly, Jim wrote that he had enrolled at the University of Delaware and intended to take as many courses each semester as his Army duties would allow. The University agreed to accept his Randolph Macon credits, and Jim was intensely focused on earning his Bachelor's Degree.

Jim also got up his nerve and wrote Carolyn that he wanted to marry her someday, after he completed college and secured another job. He said he hoped she would "wait that long for him because she was the person he wanted to spend the rest of his life with." When Carolyn's next letter arrived, there was no mention of his marriage proposal, and Jim hoped that the letter's postmark meant that she had not yet received his letter. In her next letter, Jim could see by Carolyn's neater than usual "hen scratching" that she had chosen her words carefully. Carolyn wrote that she was "very touched" by his announcement that he wished to marry her, and she felt "very warmly towards him" as well. She said she thought of him every day, and that she hoped things would work out for them both in the future. Jim was only half pleased, but then he realized a proposal is not a proposal until you are really asking.

Fort DuPont had been important in protecting Delaware's coast since the Civil War. Located across the Delaware Bay from Fort Delaware on Pea Patch Island, Fort DuPont, along with Fort Mott in New Jersey, guarded the entrance up the Delaware River to Wilmington and Philadelphia. The "three forts" zone used cannon balls, and later gun batteries, to deter river traffic in wartime. But more recently, the heavy guns had been relocated south to Fort Saulisbury near Milford, and Fort DuPont's new role was that of a large military training base for U.S. Army Reserves.

As Camp Superintendent at Ft. DuPont, Jim's duties were substantial. He was the person who designed and set the C.C.C. work group schedule. Jim reported to Capt. Earle Ewing, who oversaw all eight C.C.C. Camps in Delaware, and Col. Ulysses S. Grant III, commander of the 1st Engineers of the U.S. Army. Capt. Ewing and Jim had worked together in Lewes, and Jim was convinced that Ewing and his first C.C.C. boss, Capt. Helmer Swenholt, had spoken in favor of his selection. It also helped that Jim was a Delaware native.

The day he arrived at Fort DuPont, Jim was astounded by how much the Fort had grown since his short stays before and after his Idaho assignment. The 1st Engineers, along with C.C.C. labor, were constructing brick and mortar buildings in a clean and attractive Colonial Revival style. A huge three story barracks, a beautiful theater, four NCO residence duplexes, a guardhouse, a quartermaster station, a commissary, and other structures all still had fresh paint on them. To test their skills and provide additional officer quarters, the Engineers had floated several large houses ,one at 240 tons and sixteen rooms, across the four and half miles of water from Ft. Mott, New Jersey. Ft DuPont was a full-fledged Army Base and its atmosphere was more formal and regimented than any of Jim's previous posts. This was the Army, and at last Jim was an important part of it.

"So tell me about your new assignment," Carolyn asked as she and Jim rode north from Delaware City to Swarthmore. Jim had been given a weekend pass so he could meet Carolyn's parents and enjoy some time away from his packed schedule of Army duties and college study. It was his first day off in a month, and he was in a state of wonder at being with Carolyn for a whole weekend.

"Ft. DuPont is huge," Jim explained. "We have over 300 acres with our own hospital, post office, fire department, chapel, commissary, mess hall, firing range, port and dock, parade ground, swimming pool, baseball diamond, and football field. The 1st Engineers even have a marching band, thirty-four members strong. Senior Officers live with their families in single family houses, so women and children are present at all our public events. After years of living just with men, it's a real change for me."

"Sounds like a vacation paradise," Carolyn joked.

"Well, I've never worked such long hours in my life," Jim recounted. "Haven't even seen the inside of the theater or dipped my toes into the pool. I did attend the twilight baseball game last evening, but then I returned to my desk and drafted memos until midnight."

"Do the children attend school on base?" Carolyn asked.

"No, they ride a bus into Delaware City for school. But we offer classes on base for our C.C.C. Corpsmen and Army personnel. I'm teaching an evening course now in Forestry Fundamentals and Preparation for Civil Service."

Carolyn sighed, saying, "I don't know how you do it all."

'I don't……..do it all to my satisfaction. Right now I'm just barely keeping pace with the essentials," Jim sighed back. "My first unit, C.C.C. 1224, was just transferred from Lewes to Ft. DuPont. Of course most of the fellows I worked with, like Jack Lewis, have moved on to other assignments, or term-limited out. But it's nice to work again with Capt. Swenholt and Capt. Ewing.

"So do you really work for the grandson of President Ulysses S. Grant?"

"Yes, indeed," Jim answered. "He's as fine a gentleman as I've ever met, and a real career Army man, not just a political appointee."

Carolyn was giving Jim driving directions as they headed through Chester, PA and into the college town of Swarthmore. Carolyn told Jim to slow down as they approached a huge stone house on a beautifully manicured lot at the corner of Guernsey and Thayer

Roads. They parked the Buick by the curb and walked up a stone walkway through a corridor of boxwood. Jim, ever the forester, noticed the formal rose garden across the lawn to his left, and an informal rock garden that disappeared down the hill beyond that.

"Your home is stunning," Jim whispered as they approached the front door.

Instead of opening the door, Carolyn rang the doorbell and an African-American maid in a gray and white uniform opened it. "Hello, Lilly," Carolyn said cheerfully. "It's wonderful to see you again."

"Miss Caroline, welcome home. We've all been eagerly awaiting you and this young man."

"Lilly, this is Mr. Kelley, …Jim."

"Hello, Lilly,"

"Nice to meet you, Mr. Kelley. The Brogans are in the dining room just finishing their lunch."

Jim walked into a large hallway and onto a thick oriental rug. A tall grand-father clock beside him chimed half past twelve. To his left, Jim peered into a formal living room with a baby grand piano and oil paintings, set against the largest oriental rug he had ever seen. But then he hadn't seen many oriental rugs where he'd been living. Carolyn gently took his hand and ushered him to the right, into the formal dining room. Elsie and Charles Brogan were seated near the end of a long mahogany table, set with china and sterling silver flatware. From his time at Weitlich Jewelers, Jim recognized the quality brands.

"Daddy and Mother, I'd like you to meet my friend, Jim Kelley. Jim, meet my parents, Charles and Elsie

Brogan."

"So nice to meet you, Mr. and Mrs. Brogan," Jim responded somewhat robotically, still in awe over his surroundings.

Carolyn hadn't been home in six months, so she spent the next half hour filling in the spaces of her all too sporadic letters to her parents. They wanted all the details about her students, her coaching victories, and especially news from the farm. Charles Brogan had grown up on a farm in Cecil County, Maryland, and he reveled in crop details and "chicken chatter." Toward Jim, Carolyn's parents were warmly polite, but unquestioning.

It wasn't until after lunch when Carolyn and her mother left to retrieve some clothes packed in storage, that Jim had an opportunity to talk with Mr. Brogan.

"I like to read *The Philadelphia Inquirer* every day," Carolyn's father, said, breaking the ice as the women left the dining room. "Do you have a favorite press in Delaware?"

"Yes, I try to read *The Wilmington Daily News* each morning, and I always take in the front page, the editorials, and the financial section. If I have time, I like to read the sports page as well. I'm a real fan of the Philadelphia Phillies. "

"Well, it's good to know you root for our home town nine. I always have my radio set to the weekend baseball games, and I seldom miss listening to Paul Harvey's news commentary."

As the two men chatted about President Roosevelt and the uncertain state of the nation's economy, Jim relaxed from Mr. Brogans' quiet sincerity and straight-forward style. Charles Brogan was a successful owner of his own machine tool company, and Jim had expected a more driven personality. But instead, Carolyn's father posed thoughtful questions that were in no way intimidating. He was not out to impress anyone.

Jim could easily see that Carolyn favored her 6'2" dark haired father in stature and demeanor, instead of her 5'1" blue eyed mother of French descent. Carolyn's brother, Charles Jr., who was nine years younger than his sister and a sophomore in high school, joined them for dinner that evening. Charles was dark like his father, but built like his mother. He was much more direct in questioning Jim than his parents, and asked Jim before the first course was finished "what he did for a living." When Jim replied that he was in the Army, Charles Jr. excitedly asked Jim to describe Ft. DuPont and his daily routine. Young Charles said he hoped to join the military as soon as he finished college, and the Army was his first choice.

The next morning, Jim joined the Brogan family at the Swarthmore Presbyterian Church followed by lunch at the Inglenuk. Jim found himself enjoying the elegant and relaxed pace of things, but he felt like he was in another world. Army barracks, and his own family of six siblings, had not exposed him to such refinement. Carolyn's parents were wealthy, and that reality was a terrible wonder. Jim felt lucky and cursed at the same time.

Jim was quiet as he drove back to Delaware, and

Carolyn could sense his unease. She wanted to ask him what he thought of her folks, but then withheld her question, hoping he would take the lead. Finally south of Wilmington, Jim spoke, "Carolyn, your father is very knowledgeable and kind. And both your parents treated me like royalty. Could you write down your home address for me so I can send them a thank you note?"

"Of course, I'll do it now," Carolyn responded.

At Fort DuPont, Jim didn't want Carolyn to tarry long since she had a two hour drive south to Selbyville and daylight was already fading. He gave her a tender kiss on the lips, thanked her for the weekend, and said he would write soon. "I hope to entertain you on base for a weekend, as soon as I can arrange guest housing,"Jim assured her as Carolyn's Buick pulled away.

Carolyn drove south in good spirits, glad that the initial meeting with her parents was over.

CHAPTER EIGHTEEN

The artist that lives and works consciously sees with terrible conviction.

- Jack Lewis

Cora Quillen and Carolyn were in the farmhouse kitchen secretly planning a graduation party for Odette. "I'm so darn proud of her," Cora whispered. "She's the first one in her family to graduate college, and she will make a wonderful elementary teacher."

"Are we reserving the fire hall or the church hall for the get together?" Carolyn asked.

"I think Odette's family, "people" as she calls them, will be more comfortable in the Selbyville Fire Hall. We want to have as many of them celebrate with us as possible," Cora pondered. "Do you think you can get the invitations distributed through Leonard without Odette knowing?"

"I'll sure try my best, and if Odette does get wind

of things, she knows our intentions are pure," Carolyn said. "Odette and I drafted a letter of inquiry to three school districts last night. I am hopeful that one of them will result in a job interview."

"And if Odette does receive a teaching offer, it will be a tough choice for her."

"How so?" Carolyn asked, a bit surprised.

"Well, Odette has built quite a reputation for being the most experienced broiler raiser in the County. Her broods have consistently brought the highest prices, and she's never lost a shipment."

"You mean she could earn more raising chickens than teaching?' Carolyn queried, her voice rising.

"Not even close," Cora smiled. "If Odette raises three broods a year, she'll likely make twice as much as a beginning teacher. But there are always the unknowns, and the backaches."

"That's hard to believe, but if you say so….."

"Carolyn, Odette has had an offer to go work for a larger operation where she would be guaranteed more money. She has loyally stayed with us because we hired her first. And she likes her roommate," Cora added grinning.

Cora's remark made Carolyn remember the rainy night she first met Odette around the Quillen dinner table. She had liked Odette from the moment they were introduced, and the years had only confirmed what a remarkable person Odette Wright was. Carolyn smiled recalling her complete ignorance about chickens and her amazement the first time she bit into a piece of Cora's peach pie. Now those things were second nature.

Cora set the party menu of fried oysters, chicken salad, coleslaw, rolls, sheet cake, with some peach pie on the side, iced tea and coffee, and Carolyn seconded the plan. Carolyn insisted on buying all the groceries and it was understood that Cora would do the cooking. "What do you think, about fifty people?" Cora questioned.

"Let me draw up a list of Odette's school friends and poultry men, and I'll phone Leonard tomorrow to ask for a list of family. Yes, my guess would be about fifty," Carolyn projected. "It's going to be a fun evening."

North at Fort DuPont, Jim was engrossed in the supervision of Army 1 activities. His V-2213 men, Veterans employed under the C.C.C., were busy constructing and renewing buildings and roads, laying sewers, digging wells, and doing general landscaping projects like tree planting and pruning. Each day some of Jim's men assisted the 1st Engineers in building the four brick Senior NCO housing duplexes. Even though the country was still in the throes of a depression, Ft. DuPont was booming!

As Jim spent more and more of his day behind a desk, he found himself missing the fresh air and sunshine. Quite surprisingly, his back hurt more than ever. Just that morning, he twisted the wrong way getting out of bed, and almost dropped to his knees. Oh, to have Rocco back by his side for support, both physical and clerical.

Staff meetings with Col. Grant and Capt. Ewing were a regular part of Jim's schedule, as were planning meetings with the Squad Leaders and Assistant Leaders. Each day's mail brought letters that required immediate follow-up, and there were required government reports each day, week, and month, to fill-out and forward. When Jim wasn't seated at a desk for his job, he was more often than not bent over a book in his room. Jim was enjoying his two University of Delaware courses, but he longed to have enough hours in the day, or night, "to do them justice." As he had confessed to Carolyn, he was "barely keeping up with the essentials."

When Jim's mind was fatigued, it wandered back to reanalyze the visit to meet Carolyn's parents. Jim wondered what Charles and Elsie Brogan had really thought of him? Would he ever be able to ask them for their daughter's hand in marriage after seeing the plush environment Carolyn had enjoyed growing up? Why would *she* even want to marry *him*? He truly wished he had never mentioned a proposal of marriage to Carolyn. How presumptuous he had been.

Jim had barely fallen asleep after a late night study session when he heard a loud commotion outside his room. Someone was yelling, "Fire! Fire!" Outside his bedroom window, Jim heard feet pounding down Maple Avenue which was frozen under a February snowfall. Jim's feet hit the cold floor like lightning and he threw on his pants, shoes, and a sweater. He grabbed his Army jacket and flew down the stairs to the street.

Once outside, Jim could see the red glow in the sky, two blocks away. It was the main barracks of the

1st Engineers. Jim broke out in a run like a twenty year old, his heart dreading what his feet would discover. The fire scene confirmed his worst fears. It was utter chaos. Half- dressed men shivered and shouted, while the all too few men of the Ft. DuPont Fire Company, manned their hoses and shouted orders back. Two Companies, or four hundred Engineers, lived in the multi-storied brick building that was now well-engulfed in flames. How many of them were possibly still inside?

Jim found the Fire Company Commander who told him fire fighters from Delaware City, Odessa, and Middletown were on their way. But until they arrived, the Chief was in the process of moving his water hoses to the neighboring Band Barracks and other nearby structures, to wet them down and keep the fire from spreading. In other words, the 1st Engineers' Barracks was considered a loss.

Like a man possessed, Jim scurried around the burning structure, looking for the Senior Officers of Companies A and B. Eventually, one of them found Jim, and confirmed that all his men were present and accounted for. Col Grant arrived on the scene, looking distressed while trying to convey a sense of order and authority. For two hours, bedlam reigned as more firefighters arrived, water flew, and the men's adrenalin began to fade in the freezing night air. Manpower was everywhere, and it successfully contained the fire from spreading beyond the Engineering Barracks. But for most of the Army men who could only stand and watch, it was a strange and helpless feeling.

There was no sleep for Jim that night, nor the next. He was hugely thankful that no lives were taken, but the financial loss of the Barracks was set at $100,000. One long side of the brick building was fully exposed, and the whole roof had caved in. Four hundred men now needed temporary shelter, and many had lost all their belongings.

For months, Jim's work load increased as a direct result of the fire. Reports in triplicate were required to be filed with all the proper authorities. Jim missed two weeks of classes at the University. His professors understood because pictures of the blaze made every Delaware and Philadelphia newspaper. But being excused from class did not exempt Jim from making up the work he had missed.

Carolyn read about the fire and immediately tried to telephone Jim. Her efforts were unsuccessful, but she reached a Post operator who confirmed that no one had perished in the fire. Five days later, Jim telephoned her and they talked for ten minutes, an unusually long time. Carolyn could hear the exhaustion in Jim's voice, and her heart ached for him. She sent him a care package with chocolate chip cookies, a long letter, and one of her perfumed handkerchiefs. She included a belated Valentine's card with a photo of herself that Odette had snapped.

Jim sent Carolyn a hurriedly written postcard of thanks when he received her care package. Then weeks went by without Jim telephoning or sending Carolyn one of his beautifully penned letters. At first Carolyn rationalized that Jim was still recovering from the fire disaster. But as two more full months passed without any meaningful exchange between them, Carolyn could not deny that something was wrong. Like when Rocco died, she sensed in her heart that Jim was not in a good place.

Three more weeks passed, and Carolyn tried her best to keep calm. Her instincts told her not to appear at Ft. DuPont unannounced, as she had done the year before at Redden. She understood Jim was over programmed, but his silence could not now be attributed to stress. Had he given up on her? Carolyn remembered Jim's stony silence on the drive south from Swarthmore, and her fears increased.

Just when she was at the point of taking drastic action, a formal invitation arrived in the Quillen mailbox:

Colonel and Mrs. U. S. Grant, 3rd
request the pleasure of your company
for dinner at 6:30 p.m. daylight savings time
at the Officers Mess, Fort DuPont, Delaware,
Thursday, July 2, 1936.
R.S.V.P. Dress Informal.

Jim had penned a note on the bottom of the card saying he would telephone her on Sunday with more details. She surmised he had arranged for her weekend stay in the Post guest quarters.

Uncharacteristically, Carolyn was nervous as she drove the Buick north to Delaware City. She realized she was entering Jim's new world, and she didn't want to cause any upset. She just wanted to know that he was emotionally OK. At the Ft. DuPont entrance gate, she showed her invitation and asked to see Superintendent Kelley. The young sentry was pleasant, but kept her at the gate while he made a phone call. After what seemed like forever, the young engineer-in-training strode outside the Gatehouse and approached her car window.

"Superintendent Kelley is in the Post Hospital, Miss Brogan. He asked me to give you directions to that building."

"Hospital!" Has he been injured?"

"Ma'am, I hear it's his back, but that's not official. Just follow this road and turn right at the second stop sign. The Base hospital will be right in front of you."

"Thank you, Private."

Jim's eyes brightened when Carolyn was ushered to his bedside. "Hello, darling," he said with a sheepish grin on his face. "This has been my home for the last three days and nights. I'm sorry not to be able to give you a proper welcome."

Carolyn gave him a kiss on the forehead and as much of a hug as she dared. "Are you in pain?" she asked with concern.

"The medications they've given me have finally taken hold, so this is the best I've felt in months. I really think that they will let me get out of bed and test my legs tomorrow night so we can attend Col. Grant's dinner. That's what I'm hoping for."

Jim's hopes materialized, and he moved gingerly through the dinner party, introducing Carolyn to all his superiors and colleagues. He beamed, and whispered to Carolyn that she was by far the most gorgeous figure in the room. After dinner, the group moved outside to watch the fireworks at dusk. As the sparklers boomed overhead, Jim stood behind Carolyn, his arms wrapped gently around her waist. She asked him how he was feeling, and he said "never better," and told her standing up was much better than sitting.

After the fireworks ended, the guest lingered on the Colonel's lawn to enjoy the moonrise and the musky beauty of the summer eve. Jim had positioned himself against the trunk of a pine tree and was still holding Carolyn in front of him. With terrible conviction, Carolyn got up her nerve to speak.

"I don't plan to see a lot of you the remainder of this year, but that doesn't mean that I don't love you."

"You love me?" Jim reacted.

"Of course I love you. What do you think I have been doing for the past year and a half?" Carolyn warmly professed.

"Well, hearing you say those words is mighty nice," Jim whispered back. "Carolyn, I know I said I wanted to marry you, and I still do. But I might not be able to provide for you as well as your parents have. I understand if you just want to be friends from here on out."

"Now listen here, Jim Kelley! If you think I'm going to lose the man I love because I happen to come from a family of some means, you are mistaken. Besides, my parents are rich, not me. I'm a school teacher who doesn't make as much as a chicken house manager in

Sussex County."

Jim was delighted and amazed by Carolyn's direct statement. But he loved her enough to question her grasp of reality. Wouldn't she, shouldn't she, in the end, choose someone who could provide her a home like she had grown up in.

"Our time has not yet come," Carolyn continued. "You need every hour of the day and night to do your job here and earn your Bachelor's degree. Sunday phone calls and occasional letters will have to do for now. I'm fine with that, but I can't stand not hearing how you are doing for weeks on end."

Jim was dumbfounded at Carolyn's assertiveness, and elated that *she really did love him*. Tenderly, he kissed her mouth and told her again that he loved her beyond reason. He promised to call each Sunday between four and five o'clock. As they strolled to the Post guest house, Jim noticed that there was absolutely no pain in his lower back.

CHAPTER NINETEEN

Some of the fascinations and joys of painting lie in the fact that the doing of it requires that the painter hang on, hang on until he achieves what he thought he could not do.

- Jack Lewis

Jim had just opened two short but poignant letters. The first was from his mother who had never written him a letter before. Her scrawl was easy to read, but contained misspellings and grammatical errors.

My Dear Son,
Seen in last nites paper where you were so highly honored. James it makes me feel so happy for you, as you certainly have worked so hard and you deserve all the honer that you get. I know Willie will be glad too. Take this dollar and see a picture as you need a little

pleasure as you go along too. I just don't know what too say too you but it is just wonderful as you have had so many worries along with your work.

But I do hope everything will be better for you from now on. And I am so happy for your sake. You have all of our best wishes and I hope your work will be easier for you now. Wishing you lots of success,

With love,
Your loving Mother

Jim thought it was the most beautiful letter anyone had ever written to him.

The University of Delaware had tapped Jim to become a member of Phi Kappa Phi, the Education Honorary. No doubt his mother had seen the article in the *Wilmington Daily News*. Jim wiped a tear of joy from his cheek, overcome that he had made his mother proud, and overjoyed that he had finally done it. With Carolyn's patience and constant support, he had held on. Together they had held on to each other, through phone calls, letters, and in too brief encounters. At semester's end in June, he would graduate with a Bachelors of Arts in Education and become a certified secondary school history teacher in the State of Delaware. Earning his college degree had taken him twelve years.

Jim's second letter was from the Colonel who had been his main commanding officer since Jim's early days in Mosquito Control.

Dear Mr. Kelley:

Please accept my congratulations for your election to Phi Kappa Phi which I note by the local press. I know this has meant a lot of hard work under difficulties and I am sure you deserve the distinction.

With personal regards for your continued success from an old Phi Kappa Phi, I am,

> *Very sincerely yours,*
> *W. S. Corkran*
> *Executive Officer & Engineer,*
> *State of Delaware Mosquito Control Commission*

A smile crossed Jim's face, as he recalled the letter of reprimand he and Rocco had received from Colonel Corkran during their first year at Lewes. Jim breathed a sigh of contentment, thankful that resilience and time had the power to change all perspective.

On Monday evening, June sixth, James Arthur Kelley graduated from the University of Delaware with Carolyn as his only witness. The two young lovers were giddy since Jim had just received notice that the Georgetown School District wanted to hire him. Carolyn had her fingers crossed that either an English position or a physical education job would open, and she had sent inquiry letters to both the Milford and Georgetown school districts.

Summertime was like a beautiful dream in slow motion for Jim and Carolyn. Their summer jobs allowed them quality time together. Carolyn was back at Camp Otonka as a counselor Monday through Friday, but she had her weekends free. From Friday afternoon to

Sunday evening, Carolyn "squatted" on the Rehoboth screened porch of two of her Selbyville girlfriends who were waitressing at the Avenue Restaurant. That gave Carolyn hours to spend with Jim whenever he wasn't behind the desk at the Belhaven Hotel. Blissfully, they had some privacy and the glorious sands of the Atlantic Ocean to share. For Jim, it was the first time in many years that his life had not been regimented by the Army or by the Civilian Conservation Corps. Jim had regular work hours, but compared to Ft. DuPont standards, he could have worked his desk shift blindfolded. And, to boot, he was in love with the most beautiful creature on earth, a nymph who magically appeared at the Belhaven each Friday afternoon.

One Sunday evening, Jim and Carolyn were strolling down the Rehoboth boardwalk hand in hand, enjoying the last few hours before Carolyn's departure. As they passed the Rehoboth Club House, Jim did a double take when he spied a familiar figure. It was the tall, lanky profile of Jack Lewis, without his C.C.C. fatigues, and capped in a French beret. Jack spied Jim at the same time, and the two shouted a greeting and ran to slap each other on the back.

"Well, aren't you the real artist now!" Jim exclaimed noting the beret and the beginnings of a goatee on Jack's long thin face.

"Might as well look the part," Jack smiled. "And would this be the very lady who turned your head away from Miss Hannah?" Jack teased, his memory like a hawk.

"Yes, the very same lady. Jack, meet Carolyn

Brogan, the special person in my life."

"Delighted to meet you my dear," Jack replied, grabbing Carolyn's hand and giving it a quick continental kiss. "Please come inside and see my paintings in the exhibit. On Sunday there is no admission charge."

Carolyn gave Jim a questioning "Who is Hannah?" glance as they went inside the Tenth Annual Rehoboth Art Exhibit. Jack ushered them through the one hundred fourteen painting show, stopping before his two entries. The first painting was titled "Village Corner at Leipsic" and the second "Wyatt Wharf at Bowers Beach." Jack said he had done the preliminary sketches for both during his C.C.C. days. Now that he had term limited out of the C.C.C., he had time on his hands to transpose the sketches into finished paintings. Carolyn liked Jack Lewis' use of color, particularly in the three buildings at the turn in the road of the "Leipsic Village Corner."

"You always said you'd come back to Delaware," Jim remembered. "Are you here to stay? I'm working at the Belhaven this summer and would love to join in whatever you are up to."

"I'm not sure how long I can afford to stay. It depends on Mrs. Corkran's project to establish an Art League here in Rehoboth. We are both hopeful that I can teach art classes when the Art League finds a facility," Jack explained. Right now I'm looking for any kind of part-time job in the area, but you know how that goes these days."

"Well, I'll keep my ear open for you," Jim offered.

"The Belhaven is a huge hotel and something part-time may be posted."

After Jim saw Carolyn off to camp in her Buick, he and Jack met back on the boardwalk for some catching up. Jim confessed that he was totally in love and anxious to propose to Carolyn as soon as he could gather enough finances. When Jim lamented that Carolyn's family was wealthy, Jack slapped his knee, saying, "Let me get this right. She's beautiful, rich, employed, and you are crying in your beer? Have you lost your mind?"

The two men swapped memories of mosquitoes and puppet shows until after midnight. When they finally parted, Jim hoped that their paths would cross again, because he really missed the zest for life that artist Jack Lewis radiated.

CHAPTER TWENTY

> *The infinite miracle of life is realized as one paints. It is startling when a man walks upon a scene for which he seems to have been exactly shaped, and upon which he selects a position for the composition that is right from the standpoint of all law and design.*
>
> *- Jack Lewis*

When school opened, Carolyn was still teaching in Selbyville. But before Christmas, the Georgetown School District called her to ask if she would accept a Physical Education position beginning in January since their teacher resigned and relocated when she recently married. Leaving her Selbyville students and Cora and George would be difficult, but Carolyn knew she belonged as close to Jim as possible. Six months earlier, Odette left their chicken house apartment to take a fourth grade teaching position in Ellendale, near Milford. To supplement her income, Odette planned to work for H & H Poultry in the summer months, overseeing several of their broiler sites. Carolyn was sure that Odette would also poultry "consult" on weekends during the school year. Odette had found a way to combine both her loves, and Carolyn admired her enterprising spirit. But for six months, the apartment had been empty without Odette's company and laughter. It was time for Carolyn to move on.

From the day Jim walked into his History classroom at Georgetown High School, he was in heaven. Teaching came naturally to him, and preparing his daily lessons was a joy. In either one of his two suits, all he owned, Jim looked like a movie star, tanned from his summer in Rehoboth Beach. He assisted head Football Coach, George Keen, and during practices his male charges were impressed by Jim's strength and muscle tone maintained from years of digging ditches, cutting trees, and working sixteen hour days. Many of the girls had crushes on him, and they were quite brazen in slipping him love notes. Jim could only ignore their gestures, and hope that the games didn't escalate.

The school newspaper, *The Golden Herald,* of Tuesday, September 20, 1938 reported,

> *With five new instructors on the high school faculty, Georgetown School*

has had the largest turnover for some time. All come well qualified and appear to like Georgetown and its school.

Formerly of Delmar, Delaware, Mr. James Kelley is the Senior High History teacher. He is a graduate of Laurel High School and Blackstone Military Academy. Having attended R a n d o l p h - M a c o n College, Mr. Kelley is also a graduate of the University of Delaware. This is his first year of teaching. His hobbies are reading, collecting books, and sports, especially college football and Major League Baseball. In college, Mr. Kelley belonged to the Kappa Alpha Fraternity and also the Phi Kappa Phi Honor Society. Mr. Kelley has had many experiences while working in Government Service and as a member of the Civilian Conservation Corps in Idaho and Delaware. Also he was a Camp Superintendent at Fort DuPont, Delaware. He has worked for electrical manufacturing in Philadelphia and retail business in New York City.

Once Carolyn arrived at Georgetown High School in January, the gossip mill helped stifle some of the crushes. Carolyn and Jim kept distance between themselves at school, but as the months passed, everyone recognized that they were a couple. In April, both their teaching contracts were renewed for the school year 1939-40, Carolyn for an annual salary of $1400.00 and Jim for $400 dollars more since he had more tenure and was paid for coaching football. Carolyn's coaching duties in basketball and field hockey were unpaid but expected.

On February third, not long after she arrived, Carolyn and Jim both had parts in the G.H.S. Faculty Play, *Nothing But The Truth,* a comedy in three acts by James Montgomery. Carolyn played Sable Jackson and Jim played Clarence van Dusen. Carolyn now shared an apartment with teacher Mary Ann Kregger, who was cast in the part of Mabel Jackson. Mary Ann, who went by 'Ann' to her friends, and Carolyn had fun rehearsing their parts over dinner. On a couple evenings, Jim joined them for the food and for the theatrics, which were hardly professional. Jim took a room in a boarding house close to the High School, saying that he wanted a space to himself after years of sharing the barracks with so many others.

Carolyn said a prayer of thanks that both she and Jim were working at jobs they enjoyed. The U. S. economy was still weak, but with the Army no longer a factor in their relationship, Carolyn and Jim had more control over their destiny, or so they thought.

One golden fall Sunday afternoon, Carolyn and Jim sat outside on a bench around the Georgetown Circle as Carolyn graded English themes and Jim read the newspaper. The Circle was their favorite meeting spot, located mid-way between their two boarding houses.

"What's held your attention for so long?" Carolyn asked cheerily, realizing it had been almost an hour since they had talked.

"Europe is in turmoil, Carolyn. Hitler's tanks have just rolled into Poland, and there's going to be another World War."

"Surely you don't think the whole world will make that mistake again, do you?" Carolyn countered.

"Well, I don't think Herr Hitler gives a damn about the world's welfare," Jim said with stern vehemence that reflected his distress.

Carolyn was dumbfounded. It was unbelievable to

her that people could be convinced to kill one another again. Hadn't the League of Nations been created to make sure that the Great War was the last war?

But in a few days, Carolyn's disbelief turned to horror as Britain and France declared war on Germany, while the overrun country of Poland was divided between Germany and Russia.

Jim, always the student of world history, read the newspaper each morning, trying to approach the increasing aggression as a civics lesson. He clipped out items for his daily lectures, drawing parallels to past conflicts. He asked his students to imagine what they would do if they were a Polish citizen. Jim tried to convince himself that the Germans would be satisfied when they reached the next country's border, but he knew better.

For the most part, however, their first full year of teaching at the same high school was a time of excitement and happiness for Carolyn and Jim. The Golden Knights football team compiled an unbeaten record on the gridiron. They won eight straight games, giving up only six points all season, and scoring 171 points against opponents. Days turned into weeks, happily spent as part of an exceptionally young and enthusiastic faculty.

Jim found special joy in the school's on-stage productions. Unlike his high school and army days, he now had time to take a speaking part in *Nothing But The Truth*. Since Georgetown's Superintendent of Schools, Franklin J. Butz, was the play's Director, rehearsals served as informal teacher observation, and as new teachers, Carolyn and Jim were taking the assignment very seriously. Thayer Royal, Jim's Lieutenant at the Redden State Forest C.C.C. Camp, returned to Delaware and was hired to teach Vocational Education at Georgetown High the same year Jim was employed. Thayer was co-opted to play the part of E.H. Ralston, while other female teachers in *Nothing But The Truth* were fast becoming Carolyn's friends, Mary Vinyard, Velma Hayman, Ethel Jane Scott, and Kathryn Stroup.

Each month Jim put money away to buy an engagement ring. He wanted to formally ask Carolyn to be his wife when school ended, provided he had enough money to buy a quality diamond. Jim knew his diamonds, and he knew how expensive they were. Since Jim still had wholesale jeweler contacts in New York City, he wrote and requested a price on the weight and clarity of the gem he preferred.

That spring Jim reunited once more with Jack Lewis. The two men stumbled on each other early one morning in the Family Restaurant on Market Street. Jack said he had just secured a small studio off the Georgetown Circle and was beginning to teach classes at several Sussex County locations, including one in Rehoboth. The Rehoboth Art League was progressing, and Jack hoped to become a staff member there soon. Jack chose to live in Georgetown because of its central location and because it was the County Seat. With his artist's eye, Jack became enamored with the array of architectural styles and the town's light perspective. Georgetown was big enough to be dynamic, but small enough to be quaint. The Circle with its fountain and Courthouse captured Jack's heart.

"I think you are just following my lead," Jim quipped. You seem to turn up wherever I am."

"Oh yeah? Where are you going next?" Jack parlayed. "Not to Europe I hope," Jack added, regretting the too-close-to-home joke after the words came out.

Jim and Jack parted company for their respective jobs that day, but met often for early morning coffee during the next year and a half. After that, Hitler took them their separate ways.

"Self-Portrait" by artist Jack Lewis, 1936, gouache on paper, with permission from the U.S. National Archives and Records Administration and the Delaware Division of Historical and Cultural Affairs.

CHAPTER TWENTY-ONE

In painting, the successful work of art is half the compensation. The remaining half is in this electrifying of the senses that comes with the search for the beautiful.

- Jack Lewis

Near the end of the school year, Carolyn and Jim were chaperoning a group of Georgetown students headed for a twilight swim at Oak Orchard. Jim and two other teachers were aboard the school bus with thirty-five noisy tenth graders who couldn't wait to jump into the Indian River to cool down from the unusual May heat. Carolyn would be driving her Buick to join them after an intermural softball game finished. It was late on a steamy Friday afternoon, and even the adults were looking forward to getting wet and relaxing.

Jim stood on one of the piers, his eyes scanning the swimming area for any student struggling in the water. Most of the kids swam like dolphins, having grown up near the ocean. But a few needed watching because the relatively calm waters of the Indian River encouraged some of the boys to try antics they wouldn't ever attempt in the ocean waves. "No diving off the pier," Jim shouted. "And no running, either. It's slippery."

As he looked over his charges, Jim felt the warmth of true contentment. Teaching history and being with young people every day agreed with him. It was hard to believe that his second year of teaching was almost over, and looking back, he wondered why he had ever wanted to be a military man. Blackstone Academy, the Civilian Conservation Corps, and the Army seemed very distant.

When Jim spied Carolyn hustling down the pier toward him, his happiness exploded. He wanted to scoop her up in his arms, but there would be none of that with so many students around. Carolyn took the whistle from around Jim's neck and insisted that he get wet and have some fun. Jim obliged, knowing that Carolyn was a much better swimmer-lifeguard than he would ever be.

After all the students were accounted for and loaded back on the school bus, Jim grabbed Carolyn's hand and they headed for the river to watch the sunset. They stood at the very end of the longest pier, leaning against the railing, watching the sky turn pink, then orange. Without even disturbing the tranquility of the moment, Jim deftly dropped to one knee and said, "Margaret Carolyn Brogan will you do me the honor of becoming my wife?"

Wide-eyed, Carolyn reached for the small box he was extending toward her. She opened it and saw a round cut diamond in a golden setting. She was surprisingly speechless.

"I'd like to slip it on your finger, as soon as you give me an answer," Jim whispered.

"Yes! Of course, yes," Carolyn smiled, nearly in tears.

Jim slipped the small sparkler onto her ring finger and then took as long as he could to tenderly kiss her lips. Several people down the pier from them applauded. The lovers remained at the railing until the last red glow was gone, savoring the occasion. When it was dark enough for the pier lights to glow, Jim grabbed Carolyn's hand again.

"Our journey began on Coulter's Carousel. Let's celebrate with a spin on the merry-go-round. Agreed?" Jim suggested.

"Agreed."

As Carolyn and Jim spun in circles to the melodic sound of the carousel, the whole world was their playground. They had found each other, hung on, and now it was the most marvelous sensation to be spinning in the same direction.

On Monday morning, it didn't take long for the news of the engagement to spread like wildfire through Georgetown High. Carolyn's homeroom girls, Anne Swain, Iva Short, Betty Marvel, and Norma

Roach noticed the diamond ring before first period, and during second period, they told Dot Millman, Eva Cook, Esther Sammons, and Minnie Fleetwood. They, in turn couldn't wait to tell Francis Truitt, Doris Rogers, and Ginny Walls. Once lunchtime arrived and students gathered in the cafeteria, everyone knew. In a way, it was easier for Carolyn and Jim to function at school, now that they were officially engaged.

Once summer arrived, Jim and Carolyn had time to set a course for their life together. They decided to be married the following June in Swarthmore. That would allow them another year's earnings before establishing a home. Jim returned to the Belhaven where he was promoted to Resident Manager, giving him more salary and some longer hours. Carolyn worked her last summer at Camp Otonka and joined Jim each weekend. Beside the sea, their lives were postcard perfect.

Almost. The spring of 1940 had been bloody in Europe. In April, Germany invaded Denmark and Norway. In May, Hitler's troops invaded Belgium, Holland and Luxembourg, and the British took a beating at Dunkerque, pulling out of France before Hitler's Panzers took Paris in June. By August, there was no denying that the World was at war again. Before school resumed, Italy joined the German aggressors by invading northern Africa and pushing toward Egypt. The Luftwaffe began bombing raids on Britain. Then in September, Japan joined the Axis alliance of Germany, Italy, and Russia.

At first Carolyn was unaware how world events

were weighing on Jim. She could see a change in him even before they returned to their classrooms, but she couldn't understand why he seemed so disengaged. Was he getting cold feet about their pending marriage? Was he losing interest in teaching?

Jim knew what was coming, and he didn't even want to talk about it. The last thing he wanted to do was put his thirty-five year old, unreliable back, into a uniform again. Damn that man Hitler! How could he disrupt Jim's world when he and Carolyn had their lives perfectly planned?

As soon as Jim returned to the weekly regimen of teaching and coaching, his emotional disposition brightened. There were papers to grade, tests to type, and defenses to design. But unknown to Carolyn, and perhaps even to himself, Jim's brain was plotting another course for his, ...their, lives. Ever the newspaper reader, Jim learned that the DuPont Chemical Company had recently built a plant to make nylon in Seaford, Delaware, a town about 40 minutes west of Georgetown. After telephoning the plant to see if they were hiring, Jim forwarded his resume and cover letter. Jim had spent enough time with the 1st Engineers to know how important nylon would be to any war effort.

Jim and Carolyn spent weekends making plans for their June wedding and honeymoon. Carolyn's teaching colleagues gave her a wedding shower, as did Elsie Brogan's closest friends. As the June date approached, Carolyn was glad that they had selected June 28, allowing her more than a month at home in

Swarthmore to arrange the wedding and organize her future life as Mrs. Jim Kelley.

On June 12, two weeks before their wedding, Jim wrote to Carolyn professing his love and explaining details of their upcoming ceremony. In his beautiful script, he wrote:

> *Dearest:*
>
> *It is so good to be alive, to know someone like you, to love you and to be loved by you. Sometimes I am unappreciative and then I need to stop and think. Whatever I am or ever hope to be, I cannot lose sight of the fact that you are a grand person. If I get lost in the wilderness it is due to my own shortcomings and I shall ever strive to improve myself knowing that you are my standard.*
>
> *Ruth and I arrived home at 5:15 E.S.T. and there were ten letters here for me. I am answering Frank's and Ernie's today. The others look very interesting, especially the two from the Spring Mountain House in Schwenksville and The Highland in Wernersville. I'll bring all the literature along when I see you next Thursday. Perhaps you could inquire and try to find out something more about these two places.*
>
> *I have written to your Mother explaining our plans for next Thursday,*

so I'll refer you to her letter. I hope you'll understand about not coming for dinner. However, you may look for us sometime in the afternoon. Just when I cannot say as it depends on how long we spend in Wilmington. I'll stop in Media for the license.

This morning I purchased my brown suit. It is a dark brown twill---on the order of a whip-cord, retail $25.00. I also purchased a pair of light tan gabardine slacks at $6.50, a pair of cotton seersucker slacks at $3.50, and a pair of brown and white shoes at $7.50. The clothes will be ready Friday and they are all paid for. No I did not take any money out of the bank. Howard gave me a tie and replaced the socks which I brought for the dance. He also "knocked off" three dollars from the total bill. I am also writing to Crawford today about the white suit. Here's hoping.

Last night I saw Bob regarding the transportation problem and I believe everything is arranged. I drew a picture for him of the roads and I think he will be able to find his way to Kirklyn and Swarthmore.

The X-ray and the medical advice is glaring at me on my list and since I have two hours before leaving for work, I may

*be able to do something about those
today.*

*Please, please, sweetheart, take it
easy. Everything will work out fine. My
love, always, to the dearest girl in all the
world.*

Lovingly yours,
Jim
*P.S. Should I get a hat for our trip? Yes? Dark
Brown?*

On Saturday, June 28, 1941, at five o'clock, Carolyn Brogan was wed to James Kelley while standing together between two potted palms on the large oriental rug in front of the Brogan living room fireplace. Ruthie Davis, who was now a college student, played the baby grand piano. Odette and Leonard were present, as were Jim's sister, Ruth Draper and her husband Bill. Newlyweds Virginia Eggleston and her husband Bob Morgan, were beaming in the front row. Jim's parents were driven to the ceremony from Delmar by Jim's youngest brother, Bobby. Carolyn's brother Charles Jr. ceremoniously ushered his mother into the living room before Carolyn's Dad escorted her down the staircase, across the front hall, and up to the designated altar. Carolyn wore a white lace gown and veil with simple but striking lines. She carried a large bouquet of white calla lilies. Standing tall in his white suit, Jim thought he had never seen anyone look so radiant.

Jim Kelley's and Carolyn Brogan's engagement photo taken on the steps of Georgetown High School 1940.

Wedding day photo of Jim Kelley and Carolyn Brogan Kelley,
June 28, 1941.

CHAPTER TWENTY-TWO

After the experience of painting, the mind is completely open. Sounds are heard; colors are seen; and fragrance comes to the sense of smell — theretofore unknown. Little experiences and associations become rich and significant at these times.

- Jack Lewis

For their honeymoon, Jim and Carolyn drove to the Spring Mountain House resort about thirty miles north of Philadelphia in Schwenksville. As its name advertised, the three-story, sprawling, hotel was built into the side of a mountain overlooking a scenic Pocono valley. During four glorious days, Carolyn and Jim explored each other and their surroundings.

"Isn't it strange not to have to leave each other?" Carolyn mused.

"Very strange indeed. Marriage is a good idea, but remember, you have me for a lifetime," Jim parlayed.

"I got the better end of the bargain," Carolyn smiled, letting Jim know how happy she was. They had just returned from an early morning swim and Jim had surprised her by ordering up room service brunch.

"This mushroom-scallion omelet is divine," Carolyn purred, stretching back on the silk bed pillows. "I think you are spoiling me and setting a high standard for the rest of our marriage. "

"Yes, only the best for my beloved," Jim smiled, finding it more incredible than Carolyn to find himself in such lush surroundings with his beautiful new wife.

At the end of four days of bliss, Jim paid the $38.55 bill, noticing that the $10 .00 a day inclusive rate had been reduced for the dining room meals they had missed. Spring Mountain House had lived up to its billing as *The Beauty Spot,* and the marriage was off to a magical start.

But once back in Georgetown, July and August proved to be extremely stressful for both of them. It was no one's fault except Hitler. Jim patiently took time to explain to Carolyn what was happening in Europe and how their lives could soon change. The turbulence seemed so far away and Carolyn wanted to believe that Churchill and Roosevelt would keep the war from spreading to the United States.

When Jim confessed he had a job offer pending at the Seaford Nylon Plant, Carolyn was angry. She cried and pouted, saying the world unrest had ruined their first months of wedded bliss. Jim hugged her and said he'd write Hitler a letter of complaint. In time, after she began listening more frequently to President Roosevelt's Fireside Chats, Carolyn, too, began to realize that the war was fast crossing the Atlantic. Nothing was certain but change.

On August first, Jim received a letter from DuPont saying they could only hold a Line Foreman job open for him until August fifteenth. It was decision time. Jim and Carolyn didn't sleep for two nights, even though both of them were teaching summer school. Finally Jim made the hardest decision of his life. He sat down and wrote a letter of resignation to the Georgetown School District effective August fifteenth. He apologized for the timing, and hoped that his explanation for leaving would be understood. He said that uncertain times called for drastic measures, which he regretted. Once war began, Jim said he was sure he would be drafted unless he was working in an industry crucial to the war effort. The Nylon Plant would be one of those places.

For Carolyn, the realization that Jim was leaving his dream job *for her* soon became evident. She felt guilty for cross-examining him earlier. She knew how much he loved to teach, and she prayed that he was making the right decision, for both their sakes.

Carolyn had mixed feelings about leaving teaching. She had taught school for six years, and was turning twenty-nine. Many of Carolyn's students adored her, but recently her perspective had changed. Now Carolyn wanted babies, not just a basketball team. If she and Jim, who was five years older, were ever going to have a family, the time was now. So with characteristic resilience, Carolyn began looking for an apartment for them in Seaford. She considered commuting to Georgetown and back every day, but then realized with her coaching duties, it would be a very long day. So, with great regret, she sat down and wrote her letter of resignation to the Georgetown School Board, Franklin J. Butz, Secretary and Superintendent.

During late summer and fall, the war lines became clear. The Axis powers of Germany, Japan, Italy, Rumania, Hungary, and Slovakia, were aligned against the Allies of Britain, France, Greece, Scandinavia, and surprisingly Russia, after Germany and friends declared war on the Soviets. The U.S.S. Greer, a destroyer was attacked by the Germans in September and President Roosevelt gave orders for all U.S. naval vessels to "shoot first." In October and November, the Germans advanced through Russia and set siege to Moscow. Then one Sunday morning in December, Japan attacked Pearl Harbor and President Roosevelt immediately declared war against the Axis powers. Like everyone else, Carolyn and Jim's world changed drastically.

Jim was relieved that he had completed six months at the Nylon Plant when December 7, 1941 arrived. Once war was declared, many of the men on Jim's shift immediately resigned and volunteered for military service. Jim often worked a double shift to fill in until a replacement could be trained. It was crucial that the operating line never go down, because the nylon fiber the plant produced was needed for airplane tires, parachutes, weapons parts, and specialized uniforms.

Things moved at a fast pace, and as a Foreman, Jim used every organizational and motivational skill he had learned in the C.C.C. and the Army. Every day brought new challenges. While he didn't enjoy the job as much as teaching, Jim believed he absolutely was in the right place, for his wife, and for his country.

Carolyn found them an apartment on Pine Street, on the second floor across the street from the Bank of Delaware. Being by herself without a school schedule was strange for Carolyn who was still adjusting to her new name, her new town, and her new apartment. Since college, she had always lived with another person, and on the nights Jim worked double shifts, Carolyn found herself pacing the apartment looking at the four walls. They had few possessions, and Carolyn put the small apartment in order after the first week. Initially she was bored, but later she would look back on the freedom of those early days with envy.

As soon as the Japanese attacked Pearl Harbor, lights were greatly restricted at nights. Blackout regulations meant that blinds were pulled, cars directed their beams downward, and all exterior lights were forbidden. The Seaford Nylon Plant was considered a high priority target, both for bombing and espionage. To patrol its perimeter, a Guard Force of Army personnel were hired and worked the same three shift cycles as Plant employees.

"I think it's dangerous for you to ride your bike to work in the dark," Carolyn cautioned Jim.

"Well, my small lantern makes a lot less light than our car, and besides we have to save our gasoline," Jim retorted. Carolyn and Jim had both been issued gasoline ration cards by the U. S. Office of Price Administration. Whenever she purchased a unit of gasoline, which varied in quantity as the war progressed, Carolyn handed her card to the pump attendant who punched off one of the seven units on the card. Carolyn's parents bought a new Cadillac and gave their barely used Oldsmobile to the newlyweds. Sentimentally, Carolyn missed her trusty Buick, but she and Jim were thankful for the financial support that most young couples lacked.

Jim won the discussion and rode his Schwinn bicycle to work many nights for the graveyard shift from midnight to eight a.m. He also peddled it for the "day shift" from eight a.m. to four p.m. and for the "swing shift" from four p.m. to midnight. When gasoline rationing became severe, the DuPont Company used a whole fleet of buses to transport their workers from their homes in the surrounding Delaware and Maryland communities. In bad weather, Jim would ride the bus, even though he and Carolyn lived less than two miles from the Plant.

In so many ways, the DuPont Company supported the families who worked for them. "*Better Things For Better Living Through Chemistry,*" the DuPont marketing slogan, was applied first to its workers. At Nylon Plant events, the Plant Manager would invariably speak about "the DuPont family" and how much the Company cared about the safety and health of its workers. As Foreman, Jim had to keep detailed records of any slight accident or mishap on his shift.

Major accidents or injuries were posted outside the plant on a large billboard, and the management awarded "safety prizes" such as small household appliances to all employees whenever the Plant reached a milestone date without a major injury on the job.

Carolyn found new friends quickly, helped by the DuPont social network, purposely arranged by company management. A Seaford Golf and Country Club was built not far from the Nylon Plant, with the DuPont Company contributing most of the costs. Carolyn was elated to be able to play golf again whenever she wanted, and she made friends easily on the beautiful nine-hole course. The Company built a picnic grounds in a wooded area off the Nanticoke River and held regular family outings there. Most of all, there was a pervasive familial feeling in the work setting, that community and families were paramount. While no one checked, it was expected that you belonged to a church, or at least prayed regularly for the troops and for Hitler's demise. The Plant sold War Bonds and Stamps, and purchasing them was not an option if you wanted a good evaluation.

In the early stages of the war, the news from Europe and Africa was horrible. Everyone was scared because nothing was certain. Would Japan try another air attack? Would German submarines put spies or explosive experts ashore in Delaware or up the Chesapeake towards Washington, D.C.? Would the United States be able to convert its factories fast enough to produce the planes, tanks, and equipment to weaken the Axis powers hold on Europe?

As Jim worked the night shift, he sometimes found his mind imagining the angst of the person sitting at his former desk in Fort DuPont. Surely, that person's life must be chaotic training troops double time for assignments overseas. Jim could well envision all the activity happening in Lewes at Cape Henlopen. His old stomping grounds had become "off limits" to the public, but it was impossible to hide the tall concrete towers that were being built all along the Delaware coast. Rumors were rampant that authorities had captured espionage agents north of the Indian River Inlet. Jim smiled, remembering his escapade years earlier to rescue Jack Lewis from the Slaughter Beach jailhouse.

Painter Jack Lewis heard about Jim and Carolyn's wedding and sent them a note of congratulations, saying he intended to give them a preliminary sketch of "Cherry Lane" in Georgetown as a wedding present, as soon as he could work out transportation to Seaford. Jack wrote that he was going to enlist in the Army and hoped to see them before he left Georgetown. Almost every day, Jim heard of another friend who had gone off to war. Uncertain times reigned again, and Jim could not remember a time when life had been predictable.

Preliminary painting of "Cherry Lane" in Georgetown, Delaware, 1938, watercolor by artist Jack Lewis, given as a wedding present to Jim and Carolyn Kelley. Permission from Heather Lewis and Sallie Lewis Sharpless and painting owner, Carol Kelley Psaros.

CHAPTER TWENTY-THREE

The eloquence of the brush is unique. With merely an added stroke delivered well, the character of the subject appears.
- Jack Lewis

"Mary Lou, do you think you heard something?" Carolyn asked her friend who was peering up into the sky with binoculars.

"It certainly sounded like a plane," Mary Lou Bradley said, scanning a 180 degree arc from their post high atop the fire tower. "But I don't see anything."

The two women shared a three hour shift, and enjoyed each other's company in the brisk air of the late fall 1943 afternoon. Today they had lots to talk about. Mary Lou confided that she and her husband "Brad" had just submitted adoption papers in hopes of becoming parents. Then Mary Lou became the first person after Jim to learn that Carolyn was expecting a baby in May.

"Jim says he doesn't want me climbing all these steps in a few more weeks," Carolyn frowned. Really, you might think I was having twins. I've always been hale and hearty, but I'll probably have to drop off the watch schedule because I can tell when my husband means it."

"Well it's probably best to take it easy in the first few months, since once the baby comes, I hear life changes forever," Mary Lou said with a longing in her voice that made Carolyn feel guilty.

To change the subject and share her worries about an anxious matter close to her heart, Carolyn whispered, "Mary Lou, today I received a letter from my mother telling me that my brother Charles has joined the Army."

"How do you feel about that Carolyn?" Mary Lou, ever the counselor, asked.

"Charles always said he would join the Army one day, but it sure makes me nervous for him," Carolyn said. "It's just that's he's always been my little brother, and I love him so much. And, I think I told you that my favorite cousin from Glenolden, Pa, Carson Brogan is a Navy Pilot. He's flying regular raids over Germany now. Sometimes I wonder if we are crazy bringing a child into this world that is dropping bombs on each other."

Mary Lou just nodded her head and listened to the wind whistling atop the tower platform where the two women were huddled in a blanket.

While the women watched the skies, Jim was

rallying a group of shift workers at the DuPont Plant before they took their work stations for the swing shift from four o'clock to midnight. After reminding them of all the safety precautions, Jim raised spirits by recounting the recent success of the Americans and British in North Africa.

"If our boys are giving their all, we can too! I know this week's schedule has been hard for everyone. But we can take it! I know we can!" Jim chanted. "We can take it!" Only a few of the older men on the shift recognized the "We can take it!" chant as straight from the Civilian Conservation Corps Handbook. Many of Jim's shift workers were women, newly trained by Jim to operate the "drawtwist" machines. The transition to female operators required State of Delaware legislation, since existing labor laws prohibited women from working rotational shifts. These women were homemakers, mothers, and in some cases, grandmothers. Most of them had family members in the armed services. They were without industrial experience, were strangers to shift work, and they were concerned with all the war-time woes of loved ones overseas, transportation problems, wartime shortages, and food and gas rationing. Nevertheless, Jim found the women to be excellent operators who learned quickly and paid attention to safety, quality, and production standards. Having come from teaching, where most of his colleagues were female, Jim realized he was well suited to the considerable training task. The Seaford Nylon Plant sent 1,000 men to war-time enrollments, and Jim used every foreman skill he had acquired in the Army and the C.C.C. to train the replacements. Several of Jim's former students at Georgetown High School had graduated and were now working at the DuPont Plant. One of them told Jim that he now understood why Jim had left teaching. Those few words strengthened Jim's heart for the long nights ahead in a small town supporting a big war effort.

When Jim rode his bicycle home after midnight, Carolyn greeted him with the news that his Selective Service Classification had been upgraded to 1-A again:

Local Board No 1
Sussex County
Georgetown, Delaware

Order No. 2748

Dear Sir:

This is to advise you that the members of this Local Board reviewed your case yesterday and concluded that you were properly classified in Class 1-A, with the privilege of appealing from that classification to the Board of Appeal.

When you were in this office a few days ago you signed your Questionnaire, signifying that you wished to appeal from that classification, but you requested that you be notified as to what action was taken by this Board on your employer's claim for deferment for you, as you desired to add further information to your file before it is submitted to the Board of Appeal. Upon

receipt of that information from you, we will forward
your file to the Board of Appeal.
Very truly yours,

W. Layton Reed, Clerk
WLR/W
CC: Mr. W.L. Stabler, Nylon Plant Manager, Seaford,
Delaware

Exhausted, Jim collapsed onto the living room sofa of the new red house on Phillips Street that he and Carolyn had recently bought with a sizeable down payment from Carolyn's parents. Carolyn went into the kitchen to fix them an after midnight dinner. As Jim unfolded the letter, his new draft card fell out and onto his lap. All U.S. males were required to carry their Notice of Classification card on their person at all times and display it upon request, only to be surrendered to their commanding officer upon entering the armed forces. Every six months, the Local Selective Service Board reviewed the status of any male not enrolled and often re-issued classifications. Jim had just been re-classified from 1-B to 1-A, taking him one step closer to the Army. Tomorrow he would try again to obtain his medical records from the Army Reserves verifying his crushed vertebrae that made him immobile at times. Laird Stabler, the Seaford Plant Manager, previously submitted to the draft Board a written request that Jim not be drafted due to the importance of his skills to production of nylon for the war.

Now that Carolyn was pregnant, Jim was more

determined than ever not to rejoin the Army. He knew he was contributing more making nylon and training women operators than he ever could with his weak back on the battlefield. Jim drifted off to sleep and Carolyn had to rouse him to eat something before they collapsed into bed. By war's end in August of 1945, Jim received twelve draft cards, each shifting his classification and making the point again that the times were uncertain.

The next week Carolyn received the terrible news that her cousin, U.S. Navy aviator Carson Brogan, had been shot down over Germany and was dead. Carolyn's Uncle Lesley had enclosed a news article explaining that "Captain R. Carson Brogan, son of Mr. and Mrs. Paul L. Brogan of Glenolden, had been listed as missing in action following a flight over Bremen, Germany. He was a photo reconnaissance pilot flying a P-38 Lightning plane. His body was recovered a month later and he was buried in Westerhaver Cemetery by the Germans."

Carolyn was heart-broken, and her anxiety grew about Charles entering the Army and about Jim's reclassification to 1-A.

"Darling, you have to ease up a bit," Jim implored her, one cold evening as they huddled in front of the small living room fireplace. "Remember, worrying isn't going to help your brother, and it isn't good for the baby."

Carolyn's pregnancy was going well, and she felt her energetic self. Under duress, she had stopped her watch at the fire tower, but she was making bandages, packaging medical supplies, and collecting metal and tin. She and Jim both laughed at how quickly she was gaining a tummy. Pregnancy seemed to agree with her, especially for someone who had preferred basketball over having babies.

CHAPTER TWENTY-FOUR

*And hereby I should like to set my
life---moving from one scene to
the next and finding wonder in
all.*

- Jack Lewis

*The Hill School
Pottstown, Pa.
June 2, 1944*

Dear Carolyn---

*Congratulations! And aren't you the proud parents?
I must admit I'm jealous---started your family after I did--
-and you're ahead of me already! And twin girls---I can
think of nothing better.*

*How are you by now? Feeling O.K., I hope, and how
are the babies? I suppose they really haven't started
to gain back any weight yet. Barbie was fairly slow*

though, so I'm no judge for that. Do they look alike? Do they look at all like either of you? etc, etc. …There are millions of questions and you must know I'm consumed with curiosity---so tell me all about you, the babies, etc.

We had quite a bit of excitement here on Tuesday night---a fire started in the basement of the Library---an old storage room and got no further, but the smoke was terrific! It seemed for a while as if there really might be quite a bit of damage done---but the smoke was the worst part of it.

Where does Jim stand now in the draft? Does he come up again in June? Certainly hope he can get another deferment. Guess you know that Bob is 4-F. Had his physical February 22, and finally found out ten days later after more tests that he was 4F—kidney condition---he's been taking various pills etc. and it looks at present as if a vitamin compound has cleared it up, and I'm glad of that. But now we wonder when and if they'll review his case. Time will tell, although there seems to be a chance that he'd get 2A status now.

Are you heading back to Seaford next or to Swarthmore for a while? Would there happen to be anything I might have that you can't get because of the war? Don't hesitate to ask.

And now I must to work. Write me when you feel up to it. Our summer address: Hill School Camp, Wolfeboro, New Hampshire.

As ever,
Virginia

Carolyn received Virginia's letter on June 7, 1944, one day after the D-Day Allied invasions of Normandy began. Much to Carolyn and Jim's surprise, given the male to female ratio within their gene pool, Carolyn gave birth to twin girls on May 26, 1944. Jim insisted on naming the first girl born "Carol" after her mother, and Carolyn gave her the middle name "Carson" after her recently deceased cousin. After much discussion, the second girl baby was named "Joan Evans Kelley," the "J" being for "Jim" and the "Evans" for a man who had been exceedingly kind to Jim in Philadelphia during the depression when he was enrolled at the Peirce School. Soon Jim would have not one, but two little girls, like the little girl he saw playing in the large fountain at Washington Square in New York City in 1933. Jim counted his blessings for all the good things the last ten years had brought him.

During the hot summer of 1944, as Carolyn and Jim worked creatively to secure supplies for two colicky newborns, the Allies pushed southward from the Cherbourg Peninsula, and by August liberated Paris with help from French troops who streamed northward. By September, the Allies reclaimed Belgium, Holland, and Luxembourg, although Axis tanks would re-enter Belguim and Luxembourg in December. By October, the Allies moved into Reich, captured Aachen, and reclaimed Athens. Each evening, Jim listened to the B.B.C. on the radio, praying for Allied victories. He and Carolyn were busy with baby formula and diapers, but the war, and the Seaford Nylon Plant's support of it, was ever present in their lives.

By January, the Russians continued their eastern assault, entering Germany through Poland. In February 1945, Roosevelt, Churchill, and Stalin met at Yalta, to map plans for unconditional surrender in Europe, which would not be realized until August, after both Roosevelt and Hitler died. While the war in the South Pacific and with Japan would require more time and bloodshed, Jim gradually began to see the world conflict ending. Working at the DuPont plant, Jim heard rumors of the company's involvement in the development of a powerful new weapon. If such rumors proved true, Jim imagined that the Army, as he knew it, would greatly change.

Time and providence brought Jack Lewis and Jim Kelley together once more. Jack returned from his tour of duty in the South Pacific where he again lifted spirits with his theatrics, accordion and harmonica. In the summer of 1947, Jim and Jack bumped into each other at the Bank of Delaware on High Street in Seaford.

"So we meet again, my old friend," Jim heard as he was filling out a deposit slip.

"Jack! Is it really you?" Jim blurted out, feeling a bit foolish afterward.

"None other. How have you been?"

"Congratulations! I heard you've recently joined the rest of us in married bliss. And 'kudos' on the publication of The Delaware Scene. Carolyn and I were reading our copy only last evening, and we like the way you commented on the human interest, composition, and philosophy of each painting. All the colored plates were magnificent. It's quite an accomplishment."

"Thanks. Let's get together so I can introduce you to Dorothy, my new bride. We've settled in Bridgeville, so I guess I'm once again following on your heels."

Jim smiled, jubilant to see his C.C.C. comrade looking so dapper in goatee and beret. Over the next thirty years, Jim and Jack met periodically to share news and remember old times. Carolyn enrolled in Jack's art classes, and Jack sometimes asked his former school teacher friends for counsel when he began teaching art at Bridgeville High School and at the Sussex Country Correctional Institution.

One Sunday morning, Carolyn and Jim, each with a toddler in hand, crossed High Street in front of Mt. Olivet Methodist Church. As the foursome approached the window of Manning's Drug Store, the twins squealed and clapped their hands. Carolyn looked at the Easter display in the window and cringed at the sight of the fluffy biddies, brightly dyed in shades of pink and purple.

"Oh mommy, can we take some home? Please, can we? Can we? They are so cute!"

"Self-Portrait" by artist Jack Lewis, 1988, watercolor, with permission from Heather Lewis and Sallie Lewis Sharpless, and the Delaware Divsion of Historical and Cultural Affairs.

Author Notes

As a child, I heard my parents refer to the 1930's depression as "terrible times." Then they would move quickly on to another topic before I could ask them exactly what they meant. From my juvenile perspective, I saw hungry, bored, unemployed people sitting around dinner tables with little food and no smiles on their faces.

Fast forward fifty years to when I had time to sort through my father's two scrapbooks and discover that my childlike picture of 1930's Delaware was but a skeleton of the truth. I found letters and playbills; Civilian Conservation Corps orders, badges, diaries, rosters, dinner menus; Army Reserve documents; gasoline ration cards, Selective Service cards, and Seaford Nylon Plant records. It seems depression life was harder than I ever imagined, and better than I ever dreamed. And no one sat around for too long, hungry or not.

So, I primarily want to thank my father, James Arthur Kelley, for being the historian he was and collecting everything. Without his mementos from 1926-1945, I would not have been inspired to research the 1930's Delaware scene and write this book.

What I discovered were resilient young people determined to be the best they could be in uncertain times. I marveled at young men who traveled from Delaware to Idaho to fight blister rust and returned to restore Delaware beaches and fight mosquitoes. I uncovered the vibrant origins of the U.S. poultry industry in Ocean View and Selbyville that helped insulate Sussex County farmers from bankruptcy. And I imagined myself in magical spots, now gone or greatly changed, such as Oak Orchard, Rosedale Beach, 1930's Lewes, Fort DuPont, and wartime Seaford and Fort Miles.

Most poignantly, I rediscovered the art of painter Jack Lewis, whose creations and philosophies speak so directly to the resiliency of the human spirit. Without the trust and support of Jack Lewis' two daughters, Heather Lewis and Sallie Lewis Sharpless, I would not have felt comfortable putting words into their beloved father's mouth. So, secondly, I thank both of them for their encouragement to complete the story.

Other key cheerleaders included my sweet husband Perry, our son and his family, and my twin sister Joan O'Day and her husband Jack, who read drafts and provided valuable reviews. I thank Ruth Davis, Jerrad and Kristen Steele, Peggy Hudson, Marsha Ellingsworth, George Keene, Ruby Quillen, Nell Hutchins, and Eugene Pratt for enhancing my knowledge of chickens and poultry houses. For historical resources about the Civilian Conservation Corps in Delaware and Jack Lewis paintings, I sincerely thank Ann Baker Horsey, the Delaware Division of Historical and Cultural Affairs, the Delaware Archives, Hazel D. Brittingham, Joan Marshall Thompson, Michael DiPaolo and the Lewes Historical Society.

While I know a lot about Seaford, having lived there the first eighteen years of my life, I thank Jim Blackwell, the Seaford Historical Society, and the

Seaford Museum for facts related to the Nylon Plant and the town's war effort. I also thank Stephanie Jackson, Betty Allen Washington, Tamara Jubilee-Shaw, and David Bull for their stories about Rosedale Beach. For scenes set in Oak Orchard or Riverdale and references to the Nanticoke Indian Tribe, I thank Odette Wright, the Nanticoke Indian Museum, Tom and Edna Purnell, and Becky and Bill Scarborough. Others who provided insight or encouragement in various ways include Lisa Dougherty, Barbara Morgan Gold, Mel Goldberg, my cousin Tom Draper, Norman Justice, Lillian White, Dr. Gary Wray and members of the Fort Miles Historical Society, Tim Resch, members of the Ocean View Historical Society, and members of the Solid Grounds Book Group.

Chickens and Mosquitoes is historical fiction, and therefore not every character did exactly what the story shows, but I have made every effort to have each scene be authentically representative of depression day Delaware. Locals will recognize familiar names and places, sometimes out of date, but, I hope, never out of character. Any historical errors or misrepresentations are entirely mine.

To Learn More

About the Civilian Conservation Corps

▶ Visit the James F. Justin Civilian Conservation Corps Museum website http://www.justinmuseum.com.

▶ Visit the Army Quartermaster Museum, Fort Lee, Virginia via The Enchanted Forest website http://www.qmmuseum.lee.army.mil/ccc_forest.htm.

▶ Visit the Civilian Conservation Corps Resource Page http://cccresources.blogspot.com.

▶ Read *Life in the CCC, the Civilian Conservation Corps, Lewes, Delaware Company 1224*, paper by Suzanne Woollens, available from the Archives of the Lewes Historical Society.

▶ Read *Journal of the Lewes Historical Society, Volume XIII*, November 2010, with articles describing the Delaware C.C.C. Mosquito Control Project, available from the Lewes Historical Society www.historiclewes.org.

▶ Read Chapter 6, *The Civilian Conservation Corps, We Can Take It!* from *Delaware in the Great Depression*, Images of America, R. Brian Page, Arcadia Publishing, 2005, www.arcadiapublishing.com.

About Chickens and the Delaware Origins of the World Poultry Industry

▶ Visit the Delaware Poultry Industry website

www.dpichicken.org.

▶ Read *Delmarva's Chicken Industry: 75 Years of Progress*, Delmarva Poultry Industry, Inc. 1998, ISBN0-9667618-0-4.

▶ Read *The History of Sussex County, A special supplement to the Delmarva News and Delaware Coast Press*, by Dick Carter, 1976, pages 35-36, available in reference section of South Coastal Library, Bethany Beach, DE.

▶ Visit the Ocean View Historical Complex, 39 Central Avenue, Ocean View to see an exact replica of Cecile Steele's first chicken house, c.1923. or visit the Ocean View Historical Society's Facebook page www.facebook.com/oceanviewhistoricalsociety.

▶ Read Chapter 3, *Agrarian Life*, from Delaware in the Great Depression, Images of America, R. Brian Page, Arcadia Publishing, 2005. www.arcadiapublishing.com.

About the Life and Art of Jack Lewis

▶ Read T*he Delaware Scene* by Jack Lewis, 1940.

▶ Read Jack Lewis' own account of his C.C.C. days at the James F. Justin C.C.C. Museum website http://www.justinmuseum.com/famjustin/jlewisbio.html.

▶ Read *A Brush With Fate* by Jack Lewis, Marketplace Merchandising, Lewes, DE, 2000.

▶ Visit the Rehoboth Art League to view their paintings and purchase the DVD *If you Lived Here You*

Would Be Home Now, a film about Jack Lewis and Bridgeville, Delaware.

▶ Visit the Rehoboth Art League's website, www.rehobothartleague.org and read their history page.

▶ Visit Legislative Hall in Dover, DE to view the Jack Lewis paintings around the walls of the House and Senate Chambers, or visit Bridgeville, DE to view the Jack Lewis mural on the side of the former Market Street Grocery Store.

About Sussex County, including Oak Orchard, Rosedale Beach, Camp Meetings, the Nanticoke Indian Tribe, historic Lewes, Seaford Nylon Plant, and Delaware in WWII

▶ Read *Remembering Sussex County: From Zwaanendael to King Chicken* by James Diehl, American Chronicles, A History Press Series, 2009, www.historypress.net.

▶ Read *Oak Orchard, Riverdale, Long Neck* by Aubrey P. Murray, Rogers Graphics, Inc. Georgetown, DE, 2004.

▶ Visit the Nanticoke Indian Museum, 27073 John J. Williams Highway, Millsboro, DE 19966 (302)945-7022, or visit the DE Nanticoke Indian Tribe website, www.nanticokeindians.org.

▶ Read *Lantern on Lewes*, Where the Past is Present, by Hazel D. Brittingham,1998, available from the Lewes Historical Society www.historiclewes.org.

▶ Read *Delaware in the Great Depression*, by R.

Brian Page, Images of America, Arcadia Publishing, 2005, www.arcadiapublishing.com.

▶ Visit Battery 519 at Fort Miles, Cape Henlopen State Park, Lewes, Delaware and their website, www.fortmilesha.org.

▶ Visit Fort DuPont State Park south of Delaware City by calling the park office (302)834-7941 to secure visitor information, and read about Fort DuPont at website of Delaware Division of Parks and Recreation, www.destateparks.com.

▶ Read *Fort DuPont* by Brendan Mackie, Peter K. Morrill, and Laura M. Lee, Images of America, Arcadia Publishing, 2011, www.arcadiapublishing.com.

▶ Read *I Remember When*: The World War Periods at Home and Abroad, University of Delaware Continuing Education, 1981.

▶ Read *Memories of Frankford*, November 2003, The Memories Group, Frankford Library, available in the South Coastal Library, Bethany Beach, DE 19930.

▶ Read *Fort Miles*, by Dr. Gary Wray and Lee Jennings, Images of America, Arcadia Publishing, 2005, www.arcadiapublishing.com.

▶ Read *Seaford, Delaware*, Shannon Willey, Images of America, Arcadia Publishing, 1999, www.arcadiapublishing.com.

▶ Read *Delaware in World War II*, by Peter F. Slavin and Timothy A. Slavin, Images of America, Arcadia Publishing, 2004, www.arcadiapublishing.com.

▶ Read *Delaware A Guide to the First State*, Compiled and Written by the Federal Writers' Project of the Works Progress Administration for the State of

Delaware, 1938, American Guide Series, Viking Press, New York, available through the Delaware Heritage Press, Delaware Archives, Dover, Delaware http:// archives.delaware.gov.

▶ Read *Delaware: A Guide To The First State*, compiled and written by the Federal Writers' Project of the Works Progress Administration for the State of Delaware, 1938, Delaware Heritage Press, available through the Delaware Public Archives, 121 Duke of York Street, Dover, DE, 19901, http://archives.delaware.gov ISBN :0-924117-29-X.

▶ Visit the Seaford Museum, 203 High Street, Seaford, DE 19973, (302)628-9828, www. seafordhistoricalsociety.com.